TERROR UNFOLDING-RUNAWAY

Dolores Christian

ISBN: 978-0-9992607-9-1

CONTENTS

CHAPTER 1~LEFT BEHIND

Genoa, Italy 1990.

A slick stranger with eyes as cold as steel and lying lips lured Pearl, a Genoese runaway, into a web of crime, so she must outsmart her captor and resume her search for her mother.

"You have no choice," the stranger whispered, his breath hot against her ear. "Your father's life hangs in the balance. If you run, he dies."

"I won't let fear dictate my fate," she whispered to the night. "My mother's absence won't define me, and my father's life won't be a bargaining chip. In the back of her mind, Pearl imagined the authorities would find her dead in a dimly lit alleyway in the city. But for now, her memories of long ago kept reoccurring.

Pearl's mother, Bella, vanished from their home when Pearl was nine years old. In her absence, Pearl's father, Alfredo, took charge of her life. His actions were far from nurturing. Pearl endured countless brutal beatings, each one pushing her closer to the edge. It left her battered and broken, but it also ignited a fierce determination within her soul.

Pearl knew she had to escape her father's house, before wrath consumed her entirely in this horror house. Her mother's face haunted her dreams, a flicker of hope in the darkness, hope seemed distant, fading like a dying star.

In the tangled threads of fate, she weaved her destiny as a seeker of truth and a daughter who refused to let the darkness consume her soul.

Pearl's story resonates with the raw emotions of

struggle, loss, and the yearning for change. The past clings to her like a heavy shroud, and the universe seems indifferent to her pain. Within her words lies a desire to break free from the cycle of fear and despair.

"Resilience," Pearl said. "That allows us to withstand life's storms; it's a two-edged sword. It shields us from the blows of adversity and becomes our weapon when we choose to fight back. But now, I stand at a crossroads, contemplating a leap into the unknown.

"What if I could rewrite my narrative?" Pearl said. "What if I could gather the remains of my shattered dreams and create something new? The path ahead is uncertain. I must find resilience—a beacon of hope. It's time to break free, to turn my crisis into a new opportunity."

And so, Pearl stands on the cliff, her tears a testament to her humanity. The universe may seem indifferent, but a quiet revolution brewed within her heart. She can remain in the shambles of her present or take that irreversible step toward change. The journey won't be easy, but it's hers to embrace. Her crisis has gone too far, too long to turn back.

~*~*~*~

"My world seemed to teeter on the edge of two realities," Pearl said, "the ordinary and the fairytale. With its delicate wings and sharp beak, the bird outside the window symbolizes the freedom I long for.

"But reality has intruded, the shrieking kettle, the tattered jeans, the fall leaves dancing outside the window. These remind me of the everyday threads that interweave my existence."

And then, the front door swung open, and there stood Alfredo, a man of contradictions.
His beard and shaggy hair hinted at ruggedness, yet his eyes held a glimmer of love.

Pearl's trembling fingers betrayed her nervousness. "What's on his mind? What will he say? What secrets does he carry in that weathered face?" Her murmurs communicated a mix of anxiety and curiosity.

Alfredo stepped inside the threshold between worlds. His gaze met Pearl's, and for a moment, time hung suspended. Was it fear or anticipation that made Pearl's heart race?

The room held its breath, and Pearl's hands clenched. The kettle's echo faded, leaving only the rustling leaves and the possibility. Her husky whisper echoed, "Oh, to taste freedom, it's what I crave—love and the courage to embrace both."

Pearl's father filled the entryway at over six feet tall, and her tummy tightened. "Dad's upset," she muttered.

"Dad entered the kitchen and removed his trench coat, which revealed a chest the size of a wrestler. He now dominated the situation as he looked through his heavy glasses. I forced a hard swallow as I scrutinized my father's Italian face, which looked pale for his nationality.

"Dad grabbed another mug and hurled it at me. A glass followed and splintered into bits, gashing my bare foot. As a fork flew my way, I leaped to my feet, raised an arm to cover my face, and swayed back and forth to avoid the more precise objects he threw. Dad took a tremendous step and knocked me to the floor.

"I screamed as Dad unbuckled his belt and brought it across my shoulders. He thrashed me with his belt, and I felt the pain in my spirit. I lost track of the number of lashes, as each one caused my eyes to flash white. I realized the beating had stopped when I heard the door swing open and shut loudly and then silence.

"My mother entered my subconscious while I was writhing on the floor, drifting in and out of consciousness. The belt left welts on my skin, and I sobbed. A parent must not display hatred toward their children. Dad insulted and beat me." Dad said, "I shared my mother's lack of shame. Those words hurt as much as the beating.

"I must get away from here or succumb to my father's mistreatment. As I weighed the two possibilities, my heart skipped a beat. I love my father, but tonight, he crushed my hope for survival. I must wait until morning to leave. I don't have the mental or physical stamina to leave my bedroom tonight."

"The front door squeaked open, and I heard footsteps approaching. Dad has returned to finish the job, I thought. Today, he'll kill me. I lay motionless with my cheek pressed to the floor as I held my breath. Is that running water that I hear?

"Dad returned to take a shower. He's singing. That's odd. Dad is not one to sing, especially in the shower. What is he so happy about? I listened with intensity. It's not my dad's voice, but I don't recognize it. Then, a loud disturbance came from the hallway.

The tension in Pearl's words sounded severe, like the air before a storm. The mysterious voice and the disturbance weaved a fearful and dangerous tale.

"Every cell in my body tingled with numbness as I waited silently. It was hard for me to stay standing. My body ached, so I steadied against the wall before pushing away, forcing it into action. I seized the opportunity, darting toward the back door.

My bare feet left bloody prints on the floor. The wind whispered secrets, blood mixed with dirt, but I didn't pause. The moon urged me forward. My breaths came in ragged gasps as I sprinted more profoundly into the woods; my heart pounded like a drum. The adrenaline masked the pain in my feet, the sharp rocks and twigs slicing into my skin.

While running, I couldn't help but wonder who that person could be. It wasn't my father, the man who was supposed to protect me. How did he know Dad wasn't home? The fear and confusion mingled within me, fueling my determination to escape.

"The night air was cool against my skin. I ran, my heart pounding, until I reached the forest's edge. Under the moon's watchful gaze, I smiled at having escaped. I waited behind trees until I assumed the intruder had left. I went back home and waited until the following morning to leave.

I vowed to break the cycle—the cycle of pain, of silence, of submission. No more bruises hidden beneath long sleeves. No more crying in the dead of night. I would find my voice, my strength. I didn't know where I'd go or how I'd survive, but I had Mom's fire burning within me.

If these walls could talk, they'd tell you what occurred today. Inner thoughts stir my emotions. Dad has clarified that he detests me. It disappointed him that his marriage to Mom didn't last, and he showed anger toward his supporters.

Pearl quivered from her punishment. Her father had overheard a rumor at the bar and believed it. She had the choice of staying a victim, but she was determined to seek a better life.

As dawn approached, Pearl made a life-altering decision. She would leave this oppressive household behind, no longer a victim of her father's anger. Before her departure, Pearl would write a letter to her father and leave it on the dining table. The words within would reveal her intentions and offer a glimpse into the pain she had endured, a testament to her
resilience and determination to find a better life.

With each pen stroke, Pearl poured her heart onto the paper, hoping her father would read it and understand her desperate need for freedom.

To the man I call Dad.
  I write this letter with a heavy heart, grappling with emotions that have long simmered beneath the surface. Our journey began in a different era when you

were more than a stranger; you were a parent I cherished, loved, and held in high regard. But now, our relationship has shifted, and I find myself addressing a man I can barely recognize. I am hurt and deeply disappointed in your changes.

Heartless is a word that reverberates in my thoughts as I ponder your transformation. Your warmth was replaced by a chilling indifference. You've wielded your power over me, transforming my existence from apathy into the target of indifference. The mere thought of you sends a cold shiver down my spine. Your once gentle voice has turned harsh, your comforting touch has become distant, and you're dismissive.

How did we end up here? It was a slow erosion of compassion and empathy. You, once a protector, now stand as an adversary, a harsh stranger who thrives on my vulnerability. I've become a puzzle to solve, an inconvenience you'd instead discard.

And yet, I stayed. Why? The answer eludes me, buried beneath layers of confusion and misplaced loyalty: obedience, an ingrained response to the authority you once held. But obedience alone cannot account for the years I've endured, the sacrifices I've made. I've put my own needs and desires aside, I've compromised my happiness, and I've even sacrificed my mental and emotional well-being for the sake of our relationship.

Our bond, a testament to the depth of my love for you, stays unbroken despite the pain. I have willingly returned to your sphere, for beneath the wounds, love persists like a stubborn flame, refusing to be extinguished. I yearn for the person you once were—the parent who shared laughter, held our secrets close, and comforted me in times of tears.

The toll has been immense, not just a wound, but a deep, aching fracture that reverberates with every breath.

The paradox of love and harm within the same heart is a constant, agonizing struggle that I bear.

So, I stand, pen in hand, pouring out my truth. I see you for who you are—a man who lost his way, leaving wreckage in his wake. I fear the man you've become, yet I cannot sever the ties completely. It's a battle between my vulnerability and resilience, the same force that compels me to write this letter.

Closure that's what I yearn for—not reconciliation but understanding. You'll read these words and glimpse the pain etched into each syllable. You'll grasp the gravity of your actions, the toll they've taken. Or this letter will fade into the void unanswered.

Your unfortunate daughter.

Later that morning, Alfredo ran his pocketknife through the seam of the envelope. His eyes scanned the message, and he placed the note back on the table and walked away.

CHAPTER 2~IN SEARCH FOR BELLA

Pearl stood at the height of her journey as the sun rose. Her heart ached with her decision, yet her resolve remained unshaken like a beacon in the dark. She yearned for a life free from violence and fear, where love and kindness reigned, a life that was her own. The morning air was loaded with promise and uncertainty. Still, Pearl, with every step, was determined to face the unknown that awaited her beyond her father's doorstep, driven by her desire for freedom and independence.

My sole purpose now is to find my mother and uncover her story. Her sudden disappearance haunts me. I must fade away, give Dad space, and grant him peace. When he returns from work this afternoon, Dad will find an empty house. I must leave before I change my mind. I know a much better future awaits me.

But this sweet, blue-eyed girl feared her own shadow. And she didn't understand that God alone could fill the emptiness she looked for in another person.

As the clock ticked, a panic grew. Pearl realized her father had stayed home for the day, a rare occurrence that filled her with dread. "I'll have to wait until tomorrow morning to escape," she said. Her face was flushed, and the fear of his violent reaction lingered in her mind.

"Loneliness, what a dangerous emotion," she uttered. "This silent plague can kill. Rejection causes damage and triggers the same result in your brain as a physical injury."

This journey will alter my life and future. I'll follow my heart, although this action may invite danger. But I am ready to face it because I am stronger than I realize.

Pearl's hands trembled as she unlocked the squeaky kitchen door, which gave way to dawn. For a moment, a gust of fresh air snatched her breath away. "Ah, freedom," she murmured. Pearl smiled and embraced independence, inhaling deep breaths of the morning air. It's a change for the better.

Pearl locked the door behind her while Alfredo slept. "The swish of the wind blowing through the trees whispers peril. Monstrous trees cast dark, shapeless shadows across the mountainside. They extend against tree trunks, creep over stones, and send chills through my spine.

"These trees have grown wild since I last walked here with Mom. I must duck and protect my facial features from these twigs or have my face ripped. I must leave the neighborhood before the sun rises.

Minutes later, the sun rose, but the clouds covered it. Her thoughts returned. I ran from Dad. I left him with a heart condition. What a painful scenario. This thought didn't enter my mind.

She had chosen self-reliance, and that triggered another issue. "I have petty cash," she whispered. "People say The Historical Center in Genoa excels with action. I can work for room and board." Pearl continued to agonize over her insufficiencies.

"Distance from Dad is what I need. I'll make it impossible for him to find me. Aunt Rose will allow me to stay with her. Oh, no, I must not give her another burden. Besides, it'll be Dad's first stop when looking for me."

Pearl moaned and groaned the entire way. A person may mistake the moan for the hum of the morning wind. Pearl faced a long, arduous journey in an unfamiliar world.

When Pearl arrived at *the Historical Center,* the sky appeared dark blue with gray clouds, and foreigners strolled the streets.

"This journey took longer than I expected. The day will soon plunge into darkness. This place takes my breath away. It's huge, with restored buildings and different merchants clustered together as far as my eyes can see." She whispered, "Where shall I go from here?"

~*~*~*~

When Pearl left home, she didn't realize that terror lurked outside her window. Her decision to leave home led her right into the enemy's trap.

Dino, a notorious criminal, spotted Pearl. "Awe!" he said. "My princess has arrived. I waited twenty-four hours for her arrival, and she's now here," he told the men standing around.

Dino had executed Pearl's escape without her knowledge but acted innocent when he approached her.

"Look what the power of the wind blew in my direction," Dino said. "Tell me, what brings you here, Amor Mio?" His dark, intense eyes showed his soul from the inside out.

"Don't call me Amor," she said. "But to answer your question, I'm searching for my mother."

Dino ignored her answer. "Trouble at home, or has someone violated your territory? Let me guess, someone ruffled your feathers, and you lost the fight. Right?"

"You're unknown to me. And what happens in my personal life is not your concern," Pearl said. She was petrified and started to leave.

"Wait," Dino said, his voice low and seductive. Dino's eyes looked her over, a mischievous smile on his lips. "Stay at my place. Come dawn, you can leave. I'm Dino. What's your name?" He asked, his grin widening.

Pearl ignored his question and didn't make eye contact. She acted street-smart, but her body trembled, and her lips quivered in fear.

"Don't plan on staying here long," Dino said. "These guys will find pleasure in you. It must strike you as dangerous. You better join me, or you'll be a delightful treat for them. After a day, you'll stop existing, leaving a fascinating tale for others to heed."

"I'm not looking for a helping hand or advice," Pearl said.

"It is in your best interest."

Pearl stared at the men leaning on the wall. Men lined the walls of this ancient building. She learned later that these men waited for Dino to choose the girls he wanted. But on this night, Dino's interest was in Pearl.

Dino advised Pearl against going to the Historical Center at night. "Nighttime arrives, and the underworld surfaces. Locals and tourists intermingle during the day," he said.

Dino noticed her fear. "Don't worry," he said. "It's my contribution to young girls. I'm on my way home, and I want to help."

She glanced around, and in desperation for an answer, fear filled her soul. I can't stay here, and I can't go with this man. I can't decide which is the most dangerous. These men here will follow me if I walk away from this place. Despite her suspicion of this older man, she knew she must go with him.

"I don't want to inconvenience you," she said.

"My job is to protect young girls from these guys." Dino was much older and a clever man. He acted concerned about young girls and persuaded her.

"I'm grateful," she said. "I'll accept your offer for a safe place for one night."

"There's no place safer than mine."

~*~*~*~

When Dino and Pearl arrived at his estate, her lips tightened. The immoral conduct engulfed her. In every direction she looked, darkness captured her innocence.

"These men here belong to me," Dino said. "If you need help, ask one of them for help.

After the introduction, Dino pointed toward the bedroom and strolled away, singing a song.

Pearl stopped dead in her tracks and listened; her eyes widened. "I heard that song on the day of my beating, coming from the shower," she whispered. Pearl turned to face Dino. "I can't stay here!"

Dino smiled. "I love this song. I named it Forever Mine."

Pearl's heart raced as she stood there, her mind racing even faster. The melody that had haunted her on that fateful day echoed through the room, and she felt a chill crawl up her spine. Dino's nonchalant demeanor only fueled her anger. How could he be so insensitive? She clenched her fists, her knuckles white, and took a deep breath.

"Forever Mine," she whispered, her voice trembling. The song's name mocked her, a cruel reminder of the past. She had thought Dino was different, that he was her refuge from the pain she had endured. But now, she realized he was just another criminal.

Pearl's gaze bore into Dino's eyes. "You violated my father's house," she said, her voice low and steady. "You invaded his home, used his shower, and left a mess in his bedroom. What kind of man are you?"

Dino's smirk widened, and Pearl's anger flared. She had to get out of there. She couldn't stay in a man's home who reveled in deception. But her legs felt like lead, and her mind was a whirlwind of conflicting emotions.

"We'll talk in the morning," Dino said, brushing her off as if her concerns were irrelevant. His arrogance infuriated her. She turned away, her resolve hardening. She wouldn't let him manipulate her any longer.

She vowed to uncover the truth about Dino. There was more to this man than meets the eye, and she was determined to reveal his secrets. The haunting melody of "Forever Mine" followed her, a bitter reminder of the tangled web in which she had become entangled. She would confront Dino tomorrow, and the truth would finally become known. But for now, she must wait, her heart heavy with betrayal and uncertainty.

Pearl stared at Dino and noticed a smirk on his face. This man deceived me; he's an evil man.

Dino grabbed Pearl's arm and guided her through the hall. Dino opened the door to a large room with beds. "Pick one," he said, turning around and leaving her standing in the doorway.

Pearl feared men might occupy the other beds. I'll choose the closest one to the door, she thought.

"It's him," she whispered. He came into our home, showered, and made a mess in Dad's room searching for valuables.

Pearl heard Dino talking to someone in the hall. She listened to their conversation with curiosity. Dino's words echoed through the walls.

"Take care of her," he said.

The click-clack of wooden shoes rang in her ears and disrupted her thoughts. A short man entered the room, "A small treat to relax you," he said with a wide smile, adding an element of danger and intrigue.

Pearl kicked and engaged in a ferocious fight until he left.

The man returned with Dino. "You must get along with this man," Dino warned, trying to tie her to the bedpost. A commotion distracted Dino when a man dropped off two incapacitated girls. The man talked with Dino, and the short man prepared a bed for the girls.

After untying herself, Pearl buried her face in the pillow. Exhausted, hungry, and fearful, she continued to plan her escape from Dino's estate at daybreak.

This fear is overwhelming. I must continue my journey. Sleep eluded Pearl until exhaustion captured her.

Tension builds as Pearl grapples with fear, exhaustion, and the realization that she must continue her journey without the man who brought her into this challenging situation. The atmosphere is thick with uncertainty about Pearl's survival.

Saturday morning, the girls detained by Dino gathered around Pearl's bed. "Missy, you made a grave mistake by coming here," she heard a voice say.

In an instant, she was sitting. She had overslept.

"You have become part of the furniture." A young girl with crimson-painted lips said.

"Did Dino force you to come here?" asked the oldest.

Pearl nodded. "No, he offered me a room for one night."

"Dino's a master deceiver," she said. "This man's ruthless, a sexual predator, a tormentor, and dishonest. He often gets enraged and is a violent man. It's tough to accept him as a human.

Pearl's situation is intense! Indeed, a precarious situation.

"Did he ask you for money?"

"No!"

"He will. Dino is obsessed with power and money and craves more. We want to report him to the authorities, but he'll kill us if he knows our thoughts. Dino refers to the police authorities as his biggest enemy. But corrupt police officers keep him well informed on police procedures and activities concerning us girls.

"Another reason we can't report him is that we can't name the honest police officers. And the sad part is that we can't escape from this place."

Breathless, scared, and weak, Pearl's eyes widened in disbelief. "I told Dino I needed shelter for one night. I'll make him take me back.

"Girl, you're naïve," the youngest one said. "Dino left town this morning. Who knows when he'll return?"

Pearl glanced around in desperation. "I'm out of here," she said with a mirthless smile. Pearl saw a hand grab her arm. In a sarcastic tone, the young girl said, "Thank God you came here. You can save us from this man."

Hostile murmur and laughter rang out. "Stop," the oldest girl said. "Let her learn by experience."

Pearl smiled with a slight quiver while tears awaited a blink.

"Does he detain you here the entire day?" She asked.

"Oh no, honey," the oldest girl said, "we're getting ready to earn our keep. We face death every day. One of Dino's men drives us to a distinct part of town, and we work till he calls it quits.

"When our shift ends, the girls in the back room replace us. This building holds twelve girls. Our room is group one."

"Why can't you walk away when they drop you off on the corner? Pearl asked.

"These guys take turns watching us. If caught trying to escape, dire consequences take place. Dino's estate is a place of gloom. You'll experience unhappiness and, yes, danger, too."

Pearl's attention fell on two girls sitting at the table. The young girl whimpered every time she turned her head.

"They're the girls brought in last night," she heard someone say.

"What's wrong with the child?" Pearl asked.

"She was molested last night," she said. "And to make matters worse, Dino considers her a sex victim."

"She's a child," Pearl said.

"These thugs with warped minds favor the younger girls."

Goosebumps sprouted on Pearl's arms.

"Well, you don't have a future here," the older girl said.

Pearl's lips parted in a fake smile.

"Dino's a clever man. If you allow him to sense your fear, you'll be in big trouble. You must tough it out and fight for your rights. If you don't win, he'll respect your courage for trying."

Another girl kept silent until now. "I saw Dino's servant come to inject you with drugs last night. If you accept the first shot, you'll become a substance abuser. They'll keep you drugged and under control. After a while, you'll beg for another fix."

Pearl thought about what she'd relinquished in exchange for freedom. And in return, she'd received this gloomy life at Dino's. But she appreciated the girl's kindness and warning.

These men degrade these girls, Pearl thought. This exploitation of life they live gives rise to slavery. They no longer recognize this labor as a shackle. And they've accepted their destiny.

"This has altered my plans," Pearl whispered. She feared spending the days alone, so she befriended the girls.

During the night, she grew weary, planning her escape from Dino's estate. She assumed she heard her mother's voice. 'Put on your smarts, girl.'

Pearl sat on the edge of her bed, and tears filled her eyes. I experienced pure agony before running away from home and landing here, from where I must now escape. Here's the sad part. No one awaits for me outside this place or at home.

CHAPTER 3~A JOURNEY TO GENOA.

New York.

Travis Steele, a young American, lost his father, Malcolm Steele, to an unsuspected death, a man he admired, depended on, and loved. His thoughts now ushered in memories of when he lived a comfortable life with his father.

My father worked hard to fulfill his responsibility to give me a secure life. I promised to follow his venture into the restaurant business.

After my dad died, I attended a seminary and learned about the Christian faith. I'm undecided whether to honor Dad's memory by opening an Italian restaurant or pursuing Jesus's lead.

The terrible weather appeared endless the following week, and Travis struggled with a decision. "Give me an answer, Lord," he prayed.

Travis strolled to the window and knew life had changed with having to make his own decisions.

"New York has had to battle air pollution in the past," Travis said, but this is the most extreme I've seen." This storm has polluted the air, and the smog has caused buildings to disappear.

I'm so angry with the weather that I'm considering attending culinary school in Genoa, Italy."

He arrived in Genoa on Monday morning. He met with Joe that morning but had to find a place to live long-term.

When we attended the theological seminary in the

US, I met Joe, who invited me to Italy. He's been a great friend and has given me solid advice that I appreciate. He treats me like a younger brother and has offered me his yacht rent-free.

Joe's a good listener and an honest guy. His caring and thoughtful ways make him a dependable friend.

Travis was eager to see Joe again.

Travis met Joe for breakfast at *The Walk-In Café,* a charming little spot with a cozy interior and a patio offering a breathtaking Mediterranean Sea view.

"This small restaurant sits between the yacht and my home, and it's minutes north of Genoa," Joe said. "I know you will be pleased with the yacht. You will enjoy eating here because it overlooks the Mediterranean Sea and has a magnificent view of mountains and ships.

"But I must warn you," Joe said. "The community comes with threats from locals. But the yacht sits vacant, and you can move in without having to wait.

Don't take the tunnel to save time. It would be best if you walked through the village.

"Avoid the narrow, seedy side streets in this vicinity, which lead to the old port. Authorities tell tourists to stay indoors at night. The natives of a particular origin take offense to your breathing. The daytime's better.

"Not a problem; I'll go around. I love to walk." Travis said.

"When we finish eating we can take a walk to the Wharf and I'll show you around," Joe said. "The culinary school is in walking distance and classes start in three weeks.

Travis's life was on the verge of taking a new turn. As a romantic he never considered the trouble which comes from pursuing love.

Three months later, Travis had settled in. An unexpected incident happened. While eating at The Walkin Café Travis spotted Pearl walking across the street. Pearl's slender body caught his attention. He watched her for a few seconds as the wind blew her long black hair and a bounce came with each step she took.

A tall male walked alongside Pearl but that didn't deter Travis from following her. His eyes stayed on her until she went into a department store and disappeared amid the crowd. He stretched his neck in search of her. Pearl stopped, and he collided with her.

"Hi," she said with a smile, her voice sweet and musical to his ears, her eyes gleaming with joy.

Travis had a warm glow on his face and returned Pearl's greeting.

He composed himself and said, "Please forgive me. Allow me to introduce myself. I'm Alexander the Great."

Pearl giggled. She fixed her eyes on his sharp and striking features, in awe of how handsome he looked in his khaki shorts. Pearl loved his devilish smile and dimple on the right side.

Travis's tight T-shirt showed off his broad shoulders. Pearl liked his physique, which tapered to a slim waist. She approved of what she saw. "Sure," she said, "and I'm the powerful Queen of Sheba."

Travis stared at Pearl's olive skin and rare dark blue eyes, which stunned him. I'm dreaming, he thought.

"Please excuse me, but the Queen of Sheba lacked your exquisiteness."

"Amusing," she said.

Travis Steele, a man with a rugged charm and a hint of mystery, and Pearl Moreno, a woman with quiet strength and a past she keeps hidden, exchanged their real names in the bustling department store. Their conversation was brief, yet it held a promise of something more.

After their brief conversation, Pearl said, "Time goes by fast. My bodyguard's waiting. I better go meet him."

"Perhaps our paths will cross again in the future,"

Travis mused, a glimmer of hope in his voice.

"I'm allowed to come to the city on Fridays."

"It's unfortunate, but my bodyguard insists on tagging along everywhere I go."

"What's with the bodyguard?"

"I'm a captive in Dino's home. And he has assigned Frankie as my bodyguard because he knows I'll have him arrested if given a chance."

Travis smiled, receiving it as a joke.

As they stepped out, her bodyguard pointed to his watch. "Let's go."

"I need a phone number to reach you," Travis said.

"I don't have the pleasure of owning a phone."

Before Travis responded, she marched away.

A flippant remark, he thought.

Pearl's bodyguard hesitated and for an instant stared at Travis with intensity.

Days became a restless blur as Travis and Pearl's paths didn't cross. Finally, they met, and he invited Pearl to join him in the city, hoping to unravel the mystery surrounding her.

Pearl promised. "If I can sneak away from my bodyguard, I'll meet you on Saturday at the same place and time."

~*~*~*~

Travis prepared for the unpredictable weather and carried a rain jacket and sunglasses on a misty day. Pearl, always one step ahead, brought an umbrella. They ventured into the heart of Genoa, a city shrouded in mystery, and experienced a day filled with unexpected twists and turns. Their journey led them to Boccadse, a place that held a significant part of Pearl's past.

"I was born and raised in Boccadse and lived here until I ran away," she said, her voice tinged with a hint of secrecy. "A rough neighborhood, but fishing is good for

families. My story is different. I lived without hope, but
that's not all there is to it."

"I'm sorry you experienced an unpleasant
childhood. You dare to look beyond what you've endured
and have faith to trust a stranger with your life experiences.

"You're a man I respect and trust. One of these
days, I'll tell you the entire story of my life."

"I'm looking forward to learning more about your
courageous life."

Pearl smiled. A hint of pink covered her cheeks. As
they strolled along the bay, Pearl pointed to a lighthouse.
"It's the fifth tallest brick lighthouse in the world."

"Lighthouses remind me of Jesus," Travis said.
"He's the world's Light and shines His light on His
people."

"I enjoy this freedom and enjoy the day by visiting
unfamiliar places, Pearl said and nestled her hand under his
arm and suggested, "Shall we venture this way? The
culinary delights of Genoa are a treat, and the locals truly
relish their meals. Imagine the pleasure of sitting in a
quaint *café,* perusing a concise menu. The aroma of
sizzling sausage, warm garlic bread, and caramelized
onions wafted through the air, teasing our appetites.

Locals enjoy their cappuccino with a panino or take
home a pizza any time of day."

"You're right," he said.

"Tell me, what's your favorite dish?" She asked.

"My most enjoyable meal is a rib-eye steak with a
baked potato. This steak's a fat cut compared to others. It's
a tender marbleized steak. A juicy and flavorful piece of
beef, tasty when grilled, broiled, or pan-fried. And with the
same delicious results, this steak is number one on my list."

"A favorite dish of Italian people includes light and
creamy spinach and ricotta gnudi in osso buco, with citrus
gremolata. Sausage pizza is still my favorite."

"I'll have to try it."

~*~*~*~

As they strolled back, they paused at a verdant park to catch their breath. Travis noticed the cool, dewy grass and exclaimed, "Hold on a moment." He unbuttoned his shirt and laid it out for Pearl to sit on, the fabric cool against her skin.

"I'm grateful for the slight breeze the Mediterranean brings," he said.

Travis lowered himself beside her, resting his head on her lap. It was a simple act, but it spoke volumes about their growing comfort with each other.

"Do you believe in love at first sight?" Travis posed the question, his voice filled with a mix of curiosity and hope.

Pearl gave him a flirtatious smile and curled a strand of hair around her finger. "I've never experienced it."

The two shared poignant moments from their past, discussing how these incidents shaped their outlook on life. They conversed in a manner that brought solace, each finding comfort in the other's words. Travis tried to engage Pearl in a political discussion, but she playfully dismissed the topic.

They enjoyed a peaceful day, watching butterflies and birds flutter around the park. Travis tried his luck by chasing a butterfly with no success.

"If you walk straight to the butterfly, it will see you," Pearl said.

"You can approach it from the back. Butterflies exist as wild creatures with a natural fear of large predators. It would be best if you crept and did not frighten them. Sudden movements can trigger an escape response."

"You must be a lepidopterist," Travis said in humor.

"No, but I read a book on butterflies and learned they flutter with freedom. It'd be a fun experience if I had wings."

Pearl turned her attention to a multicolored, graceful butterfly.

"It fans its wings with elegance and freedom. But looks so lost and alone."

Travis glanced at her; his curiosity piqued. It was intriguing how she saw the butterfly as lost and alone. He decided to keep his thoughts to himself for now.

"Next time we meet, we'll go through Genoa and discover the treasures at every corner of the historical center."

"We'll see," she replied, her voice tinged with a hint of uncertainty. Travis sensed a shift in her mood, a subtle undercurrent of something unspoken in her words. He addressed it later, not wanting to disrupt the moment's tranquility. He couldn't help but feel a pang of concern for her, his friend, as he noticed the flicker of doubt in her eyes.

"Spring invigorates me because I know summer's around the corner. Late summers bring sweltering days. By this time, I'm ready for fall. It brings in the colors of the trees: yellow, red, and brown. And what can top winter with occasional snow, giving the city a magical look?"

During their rest in the park, Travis, a close friend of Pearl's, learned that Dino, a mutual acquaintance, had detained Pearl against her will. Pearl, who had been living with Dino, described her life there, leaving unanswered questions at Travis's discretion.

"Join me on Sunday. We'll spend quality time together. I'll make sure you enjoy the day."

"I'll consider it," she said, her voice betraying a hint of uncertainty.

Travis jumped to his feet. "Have I offended you?" he asked

"Better get back before Frankie misses me."

"I'm falling for you," Travis said in a low and tender voice. You're breathtaking?"

Pearl smiled, dusted off her skirt, and sighed.

"How can I help?"

"There's no way out."

"Let me tell you a story Dad often told me," Travis said. "Eagles wait, watch, sense, and, with effortless grace, spread their wings and soar. They turn their wings into the wind and rise without flapping to gain altitude. The eagle waits on the cliff and allows the contrary breezes to lift him, but the winds ground us. "But God gives peace of mind and protection. He knows our weaknesses, but we find new strengths in Him. And at the right time, we too can escape."

~*~*~*~

Pearl shared her past pain and fears with Travis. They continued their conversation as Travis walked her back through the forest.

"When I ran away, I dismissed the notion of danger outside my home. Dino forced me to succumb to a life of despair that was impossible to escape. And I fell for Dino's deceitfulness. She gave a quick sigh.

"Freedom existed for a few hours until I stepped into his Dino's pad."

"Why can't you get away now? There's not a soul to stop you."

"You believe someone is watching us? I've concluded that getting away is impossible. As we speak, Dino's men surround us. I enjoy an hour of fresh air when Dino's out of town and Frankie's playing cards. But Frankie assigns different men to watch over me.

"Dino's men appear where least expected. At times, locals recognize me; they take this information straight to Dino for free drugs.

"Dino has little trust in me. When young gang members come to buy drugs, he doesn't allow me to make a sale if Frankie's not around to protect me."

Pearl continued to tell her story. "The day I escaped

from Dad I avoided future beatings. But if I'd known the peril at Dino's place, I might've stayed home and accepted Dad's abuse."

Pearl paused, heaved a sigh, and said, "Sometimes I blame my mother for what happened. Evil invaded our home after her departure. Dad's constant insults injured me. His ridicule came each day, and we didn't converse well."

"Mom may have gone to China, for all I know," she said.

"I'm sorry to hear such disturbing news."

"When I met Dino, he acted polite, kind, and trustworthy. He behaved as a reputable man, influencing my decision to accept his offer. I dismissed the thought of Dino having deceitful plans. He acted like a lion that caught its prey.

Dino snatched my hand and led me to his car with a grin. The touch of his hand made me tremble, and I sensed an intense corruption oozing through his skin," she said.

"When Dino approached me, I needed a place for one night. Come daylight, Dino disappeared. The girls detained by Dino pointed out the consequences of my decision. They exposed Dino's dark side, which left me hopeless."

Dino returned the following day. He explained the choices he offered. "Stay and be content, or I'll throw you in the basement," Dino said. He threatened to send me back to the gang members at *the Historical Center* and kill my dad. Problems could get worse if I try to escape.

"Who knows what might happen if I had not accepted Dino's offer? I feared the gang members more than Dino."

A silence reigned. The fear Pearl experienced in her past brought tears.

"Honey," Travis said. "I know this conversation makes you uncomfortable. It's not important to give me the details."

Pearl nodded and said, "I'm okay with having you know the details, but I've lived a stormy life. To lose my parents tormented me, but the immorality at Dino's degraded me as a woman.

"I ignored my suspicions concerning Dino and found myself in a strange place, with unfamiliar individuals, facing a challenging time as a detainee. Dino claimed his estate existed as a sanctuary for young girls. I refused to give in to Dino and his ways, and he's determined to break me.

"Dino didn't mention his underworld activities, but days after my arrival, I wanted to return home or die. Drugs, pornography, oppression, danger, disease, and misery existed in this immoral place. Men appeared from nowhere, looking like hungry cockroaches. At first, I worried these men might harm me. But Dino assigned me a bodyguard, which helped me get through each day."

She took a breath and continued. "Married men come to watch videos with the girls, resulting in disease, misery, and the demise of young ladies. The constant threat of violence makes the girls obedient and reluctant to expose their captors. These girls jeopardize their lives if they refuse to follow Dino's orders.

"We'll have to find a way to free you from that place."

Pearl nodded and continued. "The opportunity came one day to help at least one boy," she said, tears rolling. "But I ignored his inner turmoil because of my inability to inspire anyone and my lack of answers. The boy died during the night."

"Darling, addiction's an enemy to everybody. He would've made his way to another supplier. There's hope if one seeks help. Otherwise, you can't help them."

"To help somebody requires you to listen to their heart. I neglected to respond. I allowed this young man to leave without a word of encouragement. It still grips my soul.

"Amid the chaos, there's good news. Dino made me the most privileged girl in his place. Even in a corrupt environment, I received an education by reading books. I applied to learn better English because I may have to visit America to find Mom.

Travis embraced her and stared into her eyes. "Go away with me to a secret island."

"I'd go with you in a heartbeat if I knew Dino wouldn't find and kill us," she said.

Travis studied Pearl for a second. She looked fragile, and her face showed signs of pain. He felt compassion for her and said, "I'm taking on the challenge."

Pearl looked puzzled. "And the challenge is?" She asked.

Travis glanced at Pearl and winked. "I plan to break the chains of a bondservant and rescue you from these thugs."

"That suggestion won't happen."

"Why can't you call the police authorities?"

"Dino reminds us we have a debt to pay. He has warned us, girls. His men will destroy us before nightfall if we report him and they incarcerate him."

These remarks surprised Travis. Pearl's in dire danger and has relinquished her freedom, he thought. "I don't take on a new task unless I know I'll finish it. Prepare to claim freedom."

Detaining someone against their will shouts out human trafficking to me. And I know there'll be consequences if I try to rescue Pearl, he thought.

They shared their hopes and dreams in secret. Pearl and Travis agreed that their relationship meant more than friendship. Their love for each other grew. Her heart belonged to Travis, but she belonged to another.

The time had arrived to claim Pearl.

CHAPTER 4~AN OMINOUS WARNING

Travis was anxious about starting a plan of action for Pearl's getaway. "This task's dicey, but I must stay courageous," Travis whispered. This undertaking has become a volatile struggle for Pearl, and a warning comes each day. Anxiety continues to creep through my entire body as I carry on.

No doubt trouble awaited Travis this afternoon; two men jumped him as he went home after a culinary class.

Travis played the scenario over and over in his mind. These men pulled me into an alley, thrashed, and kicked me. I was fortunate to throw a couple of punches, but once on the ground, they showed no mercy. They stuffed me in the back of the car and drove to another location, and the retaliation continued, he thought.

The older, heavy-set man made his point and warned me. Don't mess with our women. Go back to your own country. If you continue to entertain our ladies, expect a more severe consequence next time,' he said.

I made a dangerous decision to rescue Pearl, and now my life teeters on the abyss of death.

I'm familiar with the pier in Genoa. It's a popular tourist attraction where the assault continued. Joe had warned me of the dangers of this location. These palaces once belonged to Genoa's wealthiest families and are worth exploring. Located near the waterfront, the Genoa Aquarium is a fantastic place for families. It brings seagoing experiences to life for children and adults alike.

Genoa's harbor, Porto Antico, plays a significant role in maritime trade. It's the second-largest seaport in the

Mediterranean. While not related to the pier, Boccadsse is a charming neighborhood near Genoa. It's known for its colorful houses, small beach, and picturesque views.

After the criminals drove off, I shifted my weight and tried to stand. The muscles in my legs ached and touched every nerve. My legs scrabbled and twitched, but they refused to obey my command to stand. I knew a burning sensation often relates to damaged nerves.

"My body burned with pain. These hoodlums might've thrown me into the sea, but they feared someone nearby might see their conduct and report the incident."

Two anglers found Travis, helped him stand, and drove him home.

"When I arrived home, I noticed bruises already covering my entire torso and legs. My body throbbed, and I let out a howl.

"I first saw these two individuals in Pearl's old neighborhood. These men disapproved of me," he whispered.

After his recovery, Travis continued his daily routine, including seeing Pearl. Travis met Joe for breakfast days later, and he mentioned his thrashing. "I'm convinced the problem will disappear if I don't take Pearl to a public place."

"I told you Pearl belongs to Dino," Joe said. "Stay away from her. Trouble will follow you if you two continue to meet."

"There're local wannabes," Travis said.

"I'll warn you one more time. Dino's aware of every newcomer in town. When you entered Pearl's life, he ordered his men to follow you."

"No, it's two native men wanting to impress the younger generation."

"They knew the exact time you'd pass the alley. And they knew you took Pearl out on a date. These men work for Dino, and they're watching you."

Travis scratched his head and gave him a sheepish smile. "These guys meant to intimidate me."

"No, they want to kill you. To save my soul, I don't know why they haven't yet. They missed their opportunity; they left you for dead."

"Why do you always contradict what I say?" Travis said, and he continued his story.

"I had the opportunity to prove my fearless spirit. I grabbed one of them by the collar and punched him. One, two, three. But the big guy landed a blow to my midsection, which made my ears ring and finished me."

Joe shook his head. "Dino's aware of your relationship with Pearl. I can guarantee you he won't stop until you're dead."

"Well, I must fight the battle to win. What doesn't kill you strengthens you."

"How unfortunate," Joe said. "Pearl might be on the brink of disaster because you desire to feed your ego."

Silence descended. This incident occurred for a reason: to end my relationship with Pearl. Joe's right, and Pearl warned me that these criminals spread throughout every corner of town. He considered the warning.

"You'll be done with school any day now?" Joe asked Travis, changing the topic.

"I have six months left. I must pay more attention to class and study with dedication. Otherwise, I may flunk the semester, but this reminds me that I must take Ms. Ellen to lunch."

"Ms. Ellen will pass you. No sweat there," Joe said, chuckling.

"She's a generous and compassionate person, but she's tough in the classroom," Travis said.

"How did you find her school?"

Dad and Ms. Ellen became good friends after my mother disappeared. They spent their vacation together, and she's a good family friend. Ms. Ellen has rewarded me with an invitation to her school.

Ms. Ellen is prepared to teach me every detail she taught my dad. She taught Dad the trade of a chef and wants to attach my name to the roster of chefs. Ms. Ellen intends to create another Gordon, James Ramsay.

"But I must finish on top."

"Inspiring," Joe said.

"Don't ruin your opportunity," Joe said.

"I'll leave it in God's hands."

"Ms. Ellen will prevent me from receiving this award if I don't get equipped. She made sure I understood the prerequisites."

"It's your responsibility to finish at the top. Tell me, what are your plans?"

"Matters are pending my decision. I may buy a restaurant in America," Travis said.

"Have you considered opening a restaurant here in Italy?"

"Ideas come to mind but have no specific plans. I have enough money to do either."

"A problem poor people might enjoy having. Keep your mind focused on your goals and stay steadfast. It'll protect you from careless ways of squandering your money."

"I have no intentions to squander what Dad has left me." Travis's father trained him in skills that brought him great fulfillment.

When they finished breakfast, Joe wished him well in his endeavor.

With no answers to his problems, Travis took a walk. "I'll go down the forbidden path and hope to find answers."

Halfway through the tunnel, the rising sun's rays reached through the entrance and warmed his back.

I can see the graffiti on the walls in the bright light. I know who lives in the neighborhood. This tunnel is sometimes the dumping place for dead people. Police keep a close watch on this tunnel. Visitors fear walking this path, it's well-known that people get robbed, kidnapped, or killed on this road. And even the locals feel wary walking alone in this location, he thought.

Travis trudged the smooth pavement and kept pace while mulling over how to prepare for Pearl's freedom.

I've noticed an SUV keeps creeping closer and closer. I can't understand why he's driving at such a low speed.

"It's weird," he said as he stepped out of the tunnel, the SUV is still inching its way. I'll take a right to test these guys' intentions.

"The stalkers have continued to follow me. I'll glance over their way to see what happens. They may be lost. Oh, no, a handgun's pointed out the window," he said.

What's with these guys? They may want to rob me, but it'll waste their time.

"Dino wants to talk to you," the gangster in a black leather jacket said. His lip curled around the words, "Get in the back seat."

Travis ignored his demand and kept his stride. I'm amazed at how trouble follows me.

The driver honked the horn to get Travis's attention.

"Dino's waiting for you."

"Who's Dino? I know it's a case of mistaken identity. And what's the occasion for wanting to talk to me?" Travis asked.

"I'll take you to him. Dino will answer your questions."

Travis sensed sweat beads underneath his clothes and bile burning in his throat. He wiped the sweat off his forehead.

"Eternal God of my soul, protect me against this danger," he said as he wiped the sweat that trickled down his face.

"I'm a nasty guy when I use force," the gangster on the passenger side said.

Travis glanced in their direction. "Sorry, but I don't

negotiate or hitch a ride with strangers."

"Get in the back seat. We'll take you to Dino," the gangster said.

"I have no intentions of going with you. But what's the reason for this meeting?"

"Dino may want to endorse your lengthy stay in Genoa."

The goon pulled back the hammer of his pistol.

Travis's fear grew. I heard the click of a gun. I'm aware of these tactics. They suggest intimidation for surrender. Lord, you must recognize my paranoia.

"I'll drag you to the car if I have to," the goon said. "I'm done with your games. If you force me to act, expect severe consequences."

"I'll meet with Dino later today or tomorrow."

"Don't be stupid!" The goon shouted.

Oh, no, I've run into a dead-end street. I need to run in the opposite direction. Travis shot a glance their way.

The passenger jumped out of the car and pointed the gun at Travis's head. The goon growled, "You've wasted enough of my time, kid. Get in the car."

It caused the hair on my neck to stand upright, and a surge pounded in my chest.

A sharp blow to the back of my head dropped me to my knees. A quick pulse ran through my body when my knees contacted the concrete. I feared this fall may have done severe damage to my knees.

The gangster yanked me to my feet. 'Get moving,' he said. The goon dragged and shoved me into the back seat of the car. My body went limp.

I heard the back car door lock. Through blurry vision, I saw the assailant return to the passenger seat. The car's wheels squeal against the concrete.

Travis moaned and asked, "What have I done to deserve this treatment?"

"Quiet," the goon said. "There are consequences for

ignoring warnings. You've continued to aggravate men in this town." He swung around, and Travis saw the butt of his gun and blacked out.

The afternoon arrived, and I regained consciousness, but my eyesight blurred. I thought I saw the clouds in the sky sway. I stood on my feet but staggered and fell as if in a drunken stupor.

"They've dumped me in this alley as a stray cat," he whispered.

Hopeless and disheartened, I turned to the sky and wondered if this was God's plan for my life. Man plans, but the Lord sets up his steps. The Lord will save everyone who calls on His name. I must trust Him with my life.

It feels as if the bone marrow in my legs is on fire. The pain surges to the tip of every nerve.

Minutes later, Travis tried to stand. But his strength had left him.

He prayed. "Lord, the shadows of the late hours have unfolded. They look bleak compared to the missing sun.

"I'm looking at a scary night alone in this alley and not knowing Pearl's safety causes paranoia." Travis moaned. "This incident may end my journey," he screamed. "But I'm not ready to die, Lord," he said.

"Dino's a malicious man. He makes the weak work for free and is intolerant of those in his way. Lord, you must end his reign of terror.

"Lord, they've hurled me between two intoxicated men. And the third one left long before I appeared. The stench is repulsive and makes me gag.

"I hear dogs bark in the distance. Will I become their next meal?"

The headlights of a delivery truck disrupted his conversation with the Lord.

"Need to get the driver's attention," he said. Travis lifted his arm to wave, but the truck whizzed by the alleyway.

"Lord, there goes the last window of hope." His voice

was faint, and his arm dropped. He glanced around to see his surroundings and groaned.

"No surprise, he ignored me. Barbed wire surrounds me under boxes, debris, and trash. I'm helpless," he said, closing his eyes. "I'll die in a sea of trash," he mumbled. Travis repositioned himself and turned to inch closer to the street. The fence prevented him from getting out into the avenue.

"Lord, I pray someone will come to my aid and rescue me." Travis tried to call out to a passer-by, but his voice failed him. He continued to pray. But his voice grew weaker. "Lord, I surrender to Your will. I've used my last ounce of energy to claw my way to the edge of this street.

Pearl cautioned me about Dino's destructive plans, but I ignored her warning during the chaos. Dino's a dangerous man."

Travis closed his eyes, his body getting colder by the minute. This incident may be the end of my life.

Then, a miraculous incident happened. Strange," Travis whispered.

"There's a warm sensation around me." He opened his eyes. "Joe," he asked, but there was no answer. Hallucinations might occur, he thought.

Travis stared at the sky. The ominous dark clouds had formed fish scales across it. "Lord, you're a faithful God. I trust you will not forsake me."

"Dark clouds produce thunderstorms," Travis whispered.

The clouds encased the sky, which may burst open at any moment. I can't change the course of this storm, but I can watch the clouds gather and wait. Minutes passed before the rain poured in sheets and pelted Travis's face, and thunder deafened him.

The winds ripped through the alley, which caused debris and unstrapped matter to careen through the air. Chunks of discarded objects missed Travis's head by inches.

Minutes passed, and the winds and heavy rains subsided, leaving Travis battered and disheveled. Travis moved his head around to see his surroundings. The winds had cleared the debris that encased him.

In a final desperate struggle for his life, Travis grabbed the edge of the sidewalk step and tugged to save himself. He slipped, fell, hit his head on the concrete, and blacked out.

~*~*~*~

On a Wednesday afternoon, he opened his eyes. "Hey, anybody there!" He shouted. "I must be dreaming, or I'm dead. And my muscles tighten every time I try to sit upright.

"Oh, I get it," he said when he saw a nurse running to answer his cry for help.

"Welcome back," she said with a smile. "It's nice when my patients yell for my attention."

"Please tell me I'm alive," he said while holding his head in his hands.

"My head's going to explode."

"Yes, your claim is legitimate," she said. "You must've had a hard fall. Do you remember what caused your fall?"

"Last I remember, I tried to stand, but my legs didn't allow it."

"I'll tell your doctor you want answers."

"Has anyone asked for me?" He asked.

"Sorry."

"I ought to call my friend and let him know I'm here."

"Who's your friend?"

"Joe Bertoni."

"If you remembered his name, you're okay, no amnesia.

"I'll give him a call after I take your vitals."

Travis slept for an hour. When he opened his eyes, he saw Joe reading a magazine on his bedside bench.

"Joe?" Travis asked, his voice hoarse.

"None other."

"Did the nurse call you?" Travis asked.

"She did. What happened to you?" Joe asked in a concerned tone.

"Dino's men rewarded me with a shellacking."

"Now you know the way they run their business. Count yourself fortunate you survived."

"These guys wanted to warn me against dating Pearl."

"Oh, sure," Joe said. "But no doubt you received the message."

"I need to get going." Travis lifted and threw the blanket aside.

"I can't occupy the space others need. Hand me my clothes."

Travis tried to fling his legs to the edge of the bed.

Joe raised his hands and said, "You may not have noticed, but you have three miles of wires and tubes connected. And the doctor will become extremely angry if he sees you trying to escape."

Travis complained, "I have a pressing mission to finish." But the battle with his legs continued.

Joe chuckled. "Sorry, but the notepad doesn't show the doctor has signed a release for you. And if you don't want to scare yourself, stay away from the mirror."

Travis lowered his head to the cushion. "Pearl is missed. Have you checked on how she is doing?"

Joe stared at Travis for a moment and mulled over what Travis had asked. "Inconceivable," he said, "I'm not crazy. What makes you assume I'd go anywhere near Dino's place to see Pearl?"

"Sorry, I'm losing my mind."

Joe is a diligent worker and fifteen years older than Travis. He influences Travis in a friendly way, but in Pearl's case, they disagree.

"I wish my relationship with Pearl existed under

different circumstances," Travis said. "But I trust God has appointed me to rescue or orchestrate her escape," he sighed.

"Sure. Whatever you trust is fine with me."

"I have unfinished business with Dino."

In disbelief, Joe shook his head and said, "You're mad? You must use common sense, man."

After the brief conversation with Joe, Travis fell asleep. After three days of sleeping, Travis convinced the doctor to release him.

~*~*~*~

Fall is a beautiful time in Genoa, Italy. The worst summer heat has faded, making way for the loveliest weather you wish to experience all year.

In Italy, fall lingers from warm-to-hot days until September, but without the humidity or the tropical nights.

A breezy and cool Saturday morning woke Travis from a deep sleep. The temperature had dropped on the yacht, so he pulled the covers over his head to stay warm.

He heard loud music. Before his release from the hospital, Travis remembered that Joe intended to spend a day or two with him until he recovered.

But Travis had rebuked him. "I'll recover without your help.

"I don't need a sitter."

"Relax, bro," Joe said. "I'm staying for a couple of days."

After nightmarish thoughts, Travis jumped out of bed. "Oh, yes, I'm familiar with Joe's music," he said. "He's trying to annoy me this morning."

Joe continued to sip his second cup of coffee as he listened to his favorite song on the radio.

"Joe!" Travis called out.

"Ah," Joe said, "I thought you'd sleep the entire day."

"You're still here?" Travis asked.

"Affirmative," Joe said. "I'm staying two days, no more and no less.

Travis looked irritated. "This loud music wears on my nerves. And disturbed a sweet dream."

"Oh, dreams. They're a source of hope and courage. Often called windows to one's destiny," Joe said.

"Take time and give them consideration."

"Awe," Travis said, "may consider your free advice." He took sluggish steps to a chair after pouring himself coffee.

"Don't procrastinate," Joe said. "Tell me what's on your mind."

Travis raised his eyes, and his lips narrowed. "When Dino's men thrashed me, I recognized Dino must take responsibility and explain why the hostility."

"An ominous action might bring you more trouble."

"I need to get it straight from the horse's mouth."

"Don't concern yourself with those matters. Get better, and we'll sit and talk," Joe said.

"I'm frustrated with life," Travis said. "They meant to kill me." His voice sounded harsh. "I need answers."

"Why allow them to finish the job?"

~*~*~*~

Late in the fall, at the end of the season, Travis and Joe ate lunch at their favorite café after a Sunday service.

After lunch, Travis met Pearl for a quick chat while Joe distracted her bodyguard.

Pearl hugged Travis and said, "I've missed you."

Before he responded, she said, "You look frail. What's wrong?"

"Oh, it's a long story," he said. "I'll give you the details, but first, tell me what's happening in your world."

"Life's hard," she said. "Every time I glance at Dino, he has a demonic look. He has taken two girls to the basement.

On another occasion, a young girl may have lost her hearing. She complained about not being able to hear. Dino punched her because she ignored his orders.

"She might've found freedom because she has disappeared. I haven't seen her since Dino punched her."

"Has he mentioned the basement to you?"

"No, but his conduct's weird. He bangs on furniture and uses bad language. He's irritated with everyone. To live under these conditions is absolute torment," Pearl said. "This ought to tell you about my stance with Dino."

"Honey, I'm so sorry I failed you."

After avoiding suspicious characters, Travis broke the news. "What I'll say next goes against what I want. But we must stop seeing each other for a while," Travis suggested.

"Why?" Pearl asked and struggled to hold back the warm tears.

"The Moreno family's well known in your hometown. It's risky to go there. Let's meet next Sunday at the Palazzo Dello Sports. I understand it's a quiet place."

"A great idea. I can meet you at 5:00 pm."

Travis agreed and glanced over Pearl's head. "I'd better disappear before someone identifies us."

The parting did not go well but ended with a quick kiss. An inner voice tells me Dino's offenses will worsen, Travis thought.

CHAPTER 5~A GREAT DECEPTION

Days after his beating, Travis still lacked the strength to get involved in any physical activity.

"Here's an incentive to get you to show interest in life," Joe, Travis's long-time friend, said. "I found a piece of property I want you to see."

"What's the deal?"

A frown formed on Joe's forehead, "I want to show you a site for a restaurant within walking distance of the beach. It does not mean you have to build there. I'm giving you another alternative."

"Where's this property?"

"I want to surprise you."

When Travis laid eyes on the property, he couldn't help but voice his reservations, "It's a fantastic location, no doubt. But my priority is to keep Pearl out of Dino's clutches. This place is a good five miles from his usual haunts."

"Travis, you're not seeing the potential on this property. It's a prime location for a restaurant, with a stunning view of the beach and a thriving local community. Imagine the possibilities," Joe urged.

"I have problems I must take care of before I buy land. I'll let you know when I decide."

"Travis, you need to decide soon. This property is a hot commodity," Joe urged, his disappointment profoundly.

"Let me know if you find another piece of property more desirable. I prefer being near the beach, more affordable, and far from Genoa," Travis said.

"And let me warn you. I've yet to decide whether to build here in Italy or go back home to New York."

"I'm aware you're slow in making a decision," Joe said.

~*~*~*~

The time had come to meet Pearl. Travis knew he had to arrive before her, but a sense of unease hung in the air. The crowded arena was a red flag, a potential danger zone. 'This event today is a shocker,' he thought, 'I must stay vigilant. There are suspicious characters lurking in every corner.'

It's the wrong time to prove my bravery. My body might not tolerate another beating.

This stadium's a dangerous place to meet Pearl. I should have considered that events do take place on Sunday nights.

Pearl fears that Dino is on the verge of doing something atrocious. We must meet in secret, away from prying eyes and potential danger.

I hope Pearl takes precautions to distract her vigilant bodyguard. I need to hold her tight and make sure she's doing well.

Travis slipped into the shadows to await Pearl. His light jacket would keep him warm until darkness arrived in the city.

When Pearl arrived, Travis gave her a big smile and a tight hug. "I'm glad you came."

With Travis over six feet tall and Pearl five-seven, he could glance above her head to study the crowd.

Pearl noticed he jingled his change in his pocket and appeared nervous. "Let's go this way. I know of a quiet place."

Travis grabbed her hand. "Let's go," he said.

Pearl received a quick kiss.

This location helped him to relax. Being away from the crowd suggested safety. The shadows of trees lined the edges of the alleyways and offered a romantic view of the Mediterranean Sea.

"Tell me, what happened to you?" Pearl asked.

"Dino's gangsters thrashed me, dumped me in an alley, and if it wasn't enough, they shot me.

"Thank God the bullet grazed my thigh. I didn't know about my injury until I regained consciousness in the hospital. I'm grateful and fortunate that my arteries and organs remained intact."

"I'm sorry my misfortune has involved you. These gangsters must've taken offense at you being in my life," she said. "But I recognize now why you're limping. Thank God you're alive. Men who have a dispute with Dino's men don't survive."

I want to surprise them when I've recuperated—an excellent reason to avoid big crowds.

"What's even worse," Travis said, "Dino knows our relationship exists."

"Impossible."

"I'm telling you; he knows."

"If he knows, why hasn't he locked me in the basement?"

Pearl took a fretful look around her surroundings. "My instinct tells me he's clueless."

"These hoodlums attacked me for unknown reasons, followed me, and knew who they pursued. No mistaken identity."

"The thought of Dino knowing our business gives me chills," and I felt the hairs on my neck rise.

Travis placed his arm around her shoulders and drew her closer to him. "I despise meeting this way."

"Dino's disposition changes often, and it's hard to know his thoughts," Pearl said.

"We need to take extra precautions when and where we meet."

"I've played by his rules," she said, "but he's the

most cantankerous person I've met. He's obnoxious, and his manners get worse each day."

"Dino enjoys riding roughshod over his men and those under him. This past week, he broke a girl's wrist when he learned she kept part of the money she'd earned. And he made another girl drink a tainted beverage, which made her nauseous. These girls have disappeared."

Pearl's gravel voice conveyed a sense of urgency.

"I hear a cry for help in your voice," Travis said. "I'm committed to helping you escape from this country. But we don't want Dino to discover our plan."

"Travis," Pearl said. "Dino controls this neighborhood. He's made it impossible for young girls to break away. Rumors say that the men who tried to rescue these girls have vanished.

"I promise I'll use all my resources to free you from Dino."

"No, Travis," she said. "A stranger is powerless to help the girls escape. If you go there, they'll spot you, and you will not survive. It's time to accept reality. Please don't go to Dino's.

"We must plan," Travis said. "Whatever happens, never admit defeat. I'll study and familiarize myself with the neighborhood before moving."

"When you get involved with Dino and his men, you're gambling with fire. Please don't become a victim."

"When fire licks at your heels, you must keep your walk steady. God will shield you from the flames," he said, smiling.

Pearl changed the topic. "Last night, I learned Dino left town for the weekend. This time belongs to us. Let's enjoy this stroll."

Travis smiled, and for a moment, his lips rested on hers. Pearl's cheeks turned a rosy color. Pearl closed her eyes to savor the awe of the kiss. Travis kissed her again, but her body tensed.

"Oh no," she said. Warm tears came to her eyes, and she tightened her hand around Travis's arm.

Travis turned to see a black Lamborghini a short distance away, with the headlights shining in their direction.

"Dino," Pearl said, and she turned as pale as a ghost.

The lights on the car flickered, and the engine revved.

"We need to go!" He grabbed her hand and pulled her into the shadows.

Travis turned around to estimate the distance between them and the car. "The car's moving fast. Run, baby, run."

Travis guided Pearl into an alleyway.

Dino's car hit the curb on this narrow trail of a road.

Travis paused until his pounding heart decreased. He watched his foe go on a mission beyond vengeance.

This maniac wants to kill us, but at the rate of speed he's driving, he'll kill himself first.

Travis heard the crush of metal. "What an idiot," he thought.

Pearl heard the clanking.

They watched the Lamborghini with the engine roaring in the ravine. Smoke covered the car. "It might explode with someone still inside," Travis said. "Maybe it's not Dino driving."

"No," she said, "No one's allowed to drive his car."

"Dino must've changed his mind and stayed in town."

"He tricked me and followed me, followed us."

"We're fortunate. This accident has made it possible to get out of town."

"It's the worst time to escape." Panic appeared etched on her face.

They looked at the smoking car, and Pearl noticed Jim running to help him. "The rest of his men will intercept our steps," she said.

"Where's the best place to hide?"

"Take me back to Dino's place. Let's use the back way, please," she said.

"It's a dangerous path, and you might get hurt with thickets."

"They won't search for us in the forest. The path leads to Dino's backyard," Pearl said. "It's the path I use when I meet you."

After they entered the forest, they stopped running, and Travis asked. "What happened to our relaxed time alone?"

Pearl gave him a disappointing glance.

"We can still go away. We'll fly out of Genoa and stay out of sight. When it's safe, we'll take an airliner to America."

"Let's go. I've changed my mind. It's a clever idea."

It surprised Travis, and he gave her a big kiss.

They noticed Dino's men walking into the forest on a mission to find them. "They must know we entered the woods," Pearl said.

"Let's go back before they catch up with us, Travis said."

A disappointed Travis almost choked on his words.

When they saw Dino's estate, Travis asked Pearl. "When will we meet again?"

"I must wait for Dino to show his dim-wittedness. When I can, I'll come to see you."

"I can wait, and you won't have to face Dino alone."

"No, I'll be okay. He'll raise his voice and use bad language. But if he retaliates against me, he'll have to tell the story and refuse to look defeated."

"Stay with me tonight."

"Dino will put the entire town on alert. After tonight, Dino will reprimand Frankie, and he'll be more vigilant next time."

Their walk to Dino's ended with a quick kiss.

Walking home permitted Travis to evaluate and pray for Pearl's circumstances.

"Lord, when I first arrived in Genoa, I stood at the crossroads of my life. I considered taking on the trade of a chef or serving you by introducing others to you, Lord. I now know your specific purpose in my life. Pearl needed help." He paused.

"Pearl has become more than a one-day flight of fancy. I want to spend my life with her. I must save her from this criminal," he uttered.

~*~*~*~

Travis visited Joe, hoping he'd offer advice. Joe listened while Travis vented his frustrations. After twenty minutes of a lengthy complaint, Joe showed irritation.

Joe strolled over to refill his coffee cup and leaned on the table. "My friend," he said.

"I'm convinced this makes you responsible for keeping Pearl safe. And I trust God can make pleasant events happen. But the Lord has given you an answer."

Travis needed clarification.

"You neglected to consider God's voice," Joe said. "They tried to kill you for having an interest in Pearl. How will this end?"

For minutes, silence ruled. Joe strolled to the window. He turned around to face Travis. "Why insist on testing the Lord?"

"I'm convinced Pearl needs help," Travis said.

"You have an enemy after you, and he won't stop until you're dead."

As Joe swallowed another sip of coffee, he said, "If you care for someone, apply yourself to the fullest to set them free, but don't hang on to them for selfish reasons."

"You have a profound way of lacing affection with arrogance," Travis said.

"People find strength and freedom when they release those they love," Joe said.

Travis shook his head. "Love doesn't die a natural death."

Joe's eyes narrowed, and as he strolled away from the window, he studied Travis. "Tell me, my friend," he said. "What makes your relationship with Pearl so extraordinary that you'd risk your life?"

Meeting Pearl came with unimaginable challenges. I found a depth of strength existing in me. A firm commitment to each other proved we can weather any storm."

Joe dropped himself onto the couch with his eyes closed and remained silent.

"A known fact is that the odds are against us. But I'm confident in my decision," Travis said. "I've learned you must be courageous and hide your fears to defeat your enemy."

Travis stared at Joe with glossy eyes. "It's hard to believe you'd ask such a question," he said. "Affection's more than an action or an emotion. It's a commitment between two people to love and respect each other. They promise they'll be there for each other, no matter what." He paused.

"I trust she's the one for me. She has changed my perspective on life, and she's everything I want in a wife."

"Accept my apologies if I offend you, but if you go to Dino's estate, you'll place Pearl in further danger. And they'll kill you this time and may kill Pearl, too."

"What if my involvement with her includes God's will? Consider it for a while. I have a hunch I'm on the right track. And leaving Pearl behind in this unsafe place is unethical."

"People may call this an addiction," Joe said. "My view of this matter is that it is hard to understand why affection and romance develop destructive patterns. The rest of the story is between you and God."

"An addiction," Travis said. His lips formed a smile.

Addiction doesn't fall under affection. I built my friendship on trust and cannot survive without this friend. If the Lord wills this, I'll continue my efforts to have Dino released, Pearl."

"Women come into our lives and, without an apology, slip away," Joe said. "Others linger for a while and leave footprints in our hearts. There's a limit to tolerating women who conspire to get their way. I'll live longer without a woman," he said, tipping his mug to savor the last drink.

Travis shot a side glance over at Joe. "Pearl's not scheming.

"Her freedom can look hopeless, and I don't have a magical solution to her problem. But it'll work out."

Joe continued to stare at him. "Why waste my time with unrequited love? I'm content with my circumstances."

With such a disparity in our outlook on life, will Joe ever welcome the stand I've taken for Pearl? He might recognize it someday, but I must strive to conquer the inconsistency between us for the good of our friendship.

Joe put his hands behind his head, leaned back in his chair, and said. "Don't you want to know why I'm bitter toward women?"

Looking at Joe, Travis said, "Sure, if you care to tell me."

"At an early age, I fell for a young girl, as you have. I trusted that she cared for me. If the occasion had surfaced, I'd have given my life for her. Without cause, she distanced herself from me. I learned she'd met her soul mate." Joe looked away to hide his pain.

"The couple moved into an apartment and married. The event shattered my heart. I refused to intrude on my past girlfriend's new life or confront her with my sentiment out of respect. I struggled to conquer my own emotions," he said.

"I still feel for her. I go to Portugal every summer, hoping to see her. And when I bump into her, anxiety hits me.

When the opportunity arises to confront her, I resist because I've kept a remnant of self-respect. I've learned to develop an intense sense of dignity and show consideration for her and her husband," he said.

"I fear your connection with Pearl might lead to unforeseen sorrow. I implore you to heed my counsel and familiarize yourself with the path ahead; you must seek wisdom from those who have returned," Joe cautioned.

"Sorry to hear your friendship unraveled. It's not relevant to my relationship with Pearl. She cares for me."

"Step back and see your involvement with Pearl from someone else's perspective," Joe said.

Travis prayed. Lord, I didn't misjudge this friendship. Please help me make wise decisions in the days to come, decisions that will protect Pearl and myself. And, Lord, I'm thankful; Joe and I share one common belief: You're a faithful God.

"Travis gave Joe a look of disagreement. I'm devoted to Pearl, and I'll stand my ground. I'll continue to seek ways to free her from a life of despair.

Joe sat up on the couch, rubbing the sleep from his eyes. "Hard to believe you said that?"

Travis gave him a confused glance.

"What makes you assume Dino cares if you have fears?

Travis turned around to face Joe.

"This trade thrives in the shadows and doesn't respect borders.

A dangerous business," Joe said.

"You take the risk of danger when you step out the door," Travis said.

Joe glanced at Travis's pitiful eyes, changed his aggressive behavior, and said. "But who values my opinion?

And God works difficulties for our good if we depend on and trust in Him."

For a minute, Travis felt courageous. "Yes," he said. "God will orchestrate the entire escape." Doubts and fears increased, but never to the point of changing his plan.

"I've offered concrete advice and have done my best. The rest is between you and God," Joe said.

CHAPTER 6~DEADLY HANDSHAKE

One wintery night in October, in a hidden valley far away from the city lights, every muscle in Travis's body twitched. The wind whispered fearful thoughts into his ear.

Travis drew the sides of his black hood closer to his cheeks. An icy chill swept through him. He tried to avoid stepping onto branches that might break and attract attention. Fear of what he might find beyond the shadows of trees fed his worries.

The moon has turned a dreary gray, and the stars hit under heavy, dark clouds. A severe storm will soon arrive and hit this vicinity. I made the reckless decision to take this dicey walk into Dino's perilous district. I did not consider my nerves.

"Lord, my shepherd and protector, I trust You'll guide me tonight," he prayed. "I'm not practicing faith when I live with negative thoughts and expect this challenge to backfire."

Travis stood behind Dino's estate, blending in with the trees. He studied the surroundings of the house where Dino held Pearl captive. The bitter wind continued to blow across this mafia neighborhood. Trees bent, and the smell of rain clung to the damp air.

"Lord, remove this fear which has come upon me." Travis continued to talk to God, his eyes wide with fear.

"Every noise I hear makes me nervous. This rescue has become a dangerous blunder. Because of the lack of time, I'm unprepared for what I might find inside. If Pearl refuses to cooperate, we'll be in real trouble." Travis glanced toward the sky and shivered.

Then, there was a loud sound, followed by gunfire and dogs barking. Travis jerked back and leaned against a tree. His shoulders protruded on each side, and he drew deep breaths.

"My legs are heavy as though encased in concrete. Fear has, for sure, squeezed the breath out of me. Get me out of here, Lord."

He pulled away from the tree and hid behind an abandoned vehicle. This undertaking is a foolish idea. I may die tonight if the dogs find me.

In silence, he prayed for Pearl's safety. "Lord don't let death come to me tonight. I fear severe consequences for Pearl if I die at this point."

A quiver at the corners of his mouth exposed his fear as he exhaled through his nose. He frowned. "No, I refuse to accept such an outcome."

Travis opened his eyes to study the setting, feet from where he hid. He analyzed the scene with shock. A man's body lay on the ground, which triggered a more significant chest-thumping fear in him.

Lord, these men dishonored life by claiming credit for killing a man. And seeing a group of callous men gather around a lifeless body is heartless.

In silence, he prayed for Pearl's safety. "Lord don't let death come to me tonight. I fear severe consequences for Pearl if I die at this point."

The rowdy conversation among these men went on for thirty minutes.

"Lord," he prayed. "They've agreed they shot an intruder. This incident is poignant. Their lack of remorse shows the severity of their heart."

Without a doubt, this tragedy triggered various questions. "What if the dead man's description fits a drifter? Mental issues could've played a part here."

"Lord, I saw a murder take place." Travis remained

motionless as thoughts clouded his mind. They could've shot me, and I'd be on that damp ground.

He studied these barbaric men as they wrapped their bodies in an old blanket. They tossed the corpse into the back of a truck as trash. They leaped into a car and disappeared into the fog.

Pearl warned me. "It's a dire risk going to a dangerous territory at night." A person with the right mind will avoid coming here after dark.

Oh, Genoa, I'm amazed at what a city can display at night. Why does a picturesque town like this harbor such evil at night?

After Travis analyzed what had happened, he abandoned his mission. In the cloak of darkness and little moonlight to cover him, he retraced his steps and slipped away, advancing with every step.

"I thank You, Lord, You're faithful to Your word. You've protected me from death tonight."

~*~*~*~

The following morning, Travis thought. What occurred at Dino's kept me awake last night. I'm trying to make sense of the whole scenario. I need answers to what I experienced. Travis remained traumatized and went to visit his friend. "Do you have a minute?" Travis asked Joe.

"It depends on what I'm giving my time to," Joe said.

Travis reached out and pulled a chair closer to Joe, looking perplexed. "I went to Dino's last night. A commotion broke out in his vicinity, and I found myself terrified. So, I canceled my plans to rescue Pearl until I'm better prepared."

Joe's mouth dropped, his head tilted sideways, and his eyes squinted in disbelief. "What? Hard to believe you went to Dino's after the warnings you've received."

Travis replied with a sheepish smile. "I intended to rescue Pearl."

Joe shook his head and spoke louder. "Value your life and attach some importance to it."

Surprised at his response, Travis remained silent.

"What makes you think that you're invincible? Tell me," Joe said.

"My concern is for Pearl. Dino has become suspicious of her activities, and she fears he might end her life."

"Maybe he wants to end your life," Joe said.

Travis described a handful of details of the event over a cup of dark coffee.

"I'm going back today," Travis said in a firm tone. "Last night, I feared, but today, I reckon we better run for our lives."

"It's an insane idea!" Joe said it in a frightening voice. To go back to Dino's may finish both your lives! Dino has a spy on every corner. I know you've heard it a thousand times. How ludicrous to imagine you can escape this country without Dino firing shots. Pearl's aware of the risk. What's keeping you from seeing the danger?"

"My affection for her outweighs any risks involved."

Full of frustration, Joe leaned on the table with his fists balled and shouted at Travis. "What can a dead man do?"

They stared at each other in utter shock. This irritated Travis because Joe had spoken to him in a humiliating way.

"Sorry, bro," Joe said, "but you've decided with your heart and neglected common sense. And there's another problem. Frankie, Pearl's bodyguard, keeps a close eye on her. You assume you can trot into Dino's place and snatch her away. What comes next?"

Travis remained silent. Joe continued. "If Dino finds Pearl's missing, he'll explode."

"When I first arrived in Italy," Travis said, "my

priorities changed from one day to another. I struggled with what I wanted to do in life. I plan to finish school before I court women, but how does one resist a gorgeous lady? To quit at this point will mean I'll return to America alone and, without a doubt, will not see her freedom."

"If you stay, you might see her death. Let me give you advice on this problem," Joe sighed.

"Don't return to Dino's turf. These men will tear and chop your heart into pieces and feed you to the dogs. Use another plan. Dino's vicinity doesn't welcome strangers."

"There's no other plan," Travis said. A worried frown crossed his face. "I'll knock on the door and face whatever comes my way."

Joe wrinkled his forehead as if to signal disapproval. "The approach you're talking about has a name. We call this suicide, my friend," he said in a low tone.

"But if I can't persuade you, I must tag along with you." A scowl remained on his forehead.

"Thanks," Travis said, "but it won't be necessary."

"I'm afraid I must insist. I have no chores for today."

"Okay, I'll enjoy the company but stay out of my way."

"It's hard to understand you sometimes," Joe said.

"I'm not a boy. I'm a grown man, and I can manage Dino." Travis glared at Joe, paused for a moment, and considered keeping the murder a secret.

But Joe continued with inquiries.

"What else happened last night?"

"I'm debating a huge decision I must make," Travis said.

"If Dino's involved, I say run. Run fast, and don't look back," Joe said. "Knowing Dino, the problem's dangerous."

Travis could no longer hold back what happened at Dino's and blurted it out. "A murder occurred last night. I'm going to fill out a report today."

"A murder occurred at Dino's. That's the commotion you heard."

Joe's eyes widened, his mouth dropped, and worried wrinkles formed on his forehead. His shoulders dropped.

"In his backyard," Travis said, "but they've disposed of the body."

"No!" Joe said. "Don't discuss this one with anyone. It'll come back to haunt you. You'd better discard the idea if you lack evidence.

"You're dead before you testify against him. Don't let incidents like this destroy your life."

Joe wiped his sweaty palms on a towel. His voice rose for a moment, and his face bore signs of panic. "Please tell me no one saw you."

"No, otherwise, you'd find me in the morgue."

That's why I rebuked you because we live in a dangerous world. The horror stories of men involved with these young girls circulate throughout the town. Human life has no worth here."

"Help me understand last night," Travis said. "You trust the man killed last night, intended to help a young woman gain her freedom?"

"Why else would he come around? Men who aren't familiar with Dino's ways will take the risk. Dino's a ferocious tyrant with power. He can make any girl disappear without a trace. And he can drop you in a blink of an eye."

Travis stared into his coffee mug and mulled over what Joe said. He feared someone died without justification, and he must report this murder.

"Somewhere, someone will miss a son, a brother, or a friend. I don't want his family to assume he's disappeared without a trace. His relatives need to know what happened to him."

Joe's jaw tightened. "I agree murder's a despicable offense," he said with wide eyes, "but you saw nothing, you hear me!"

Travis nodded. I'm afraid I must disagree with him in this scenario. But I agree that this might come back to haunt me. My moral obligation is to report this incident, even if I'm unfamiliar with his relatives.

"In my wildest dreams, I can't imagine facing death three times in less than one year," Travis said.

"Travis, I fear for your life. I discourage your relationship with Pearl because I know Dino's reputation."

"That's a waste of time, Joe."

Taking turns, Travis and Joe fixed their eyes on their cups and sipped on their coffee.

After minutes had passed, Travis looked at his friend and said, "I need Pearl's full cooperation. She's petrified and reluctant to decide, but I'm relentless. I'll fight until the end," he said, smiling.

"Relentless or brainless," Joe smiled and sipped the last lukewarm dregs of his coffee.

~*~*~*~

The following Saturday, on another frosty morning in Genoa, Travis made his way to visit Pearl at Dino's. Joe went with him.

Dino's front yard appeared desolate, with no signs that anyone lived there.

"The place feels eerie, and the odor's offensive. I'm uncomfortable in my boots," Joe said faintly.

As they reached the stairs leading to Dino's front door, Travis said, "You smell the stink of death."

Travis sensed someone lying in wait. "Stay here," he told Joe. Travis raised his eyes to survey the two-story estate, hoping to glimpse Pearl on the terrace. Instead, a diminutive man stared at them from the upstairs window.

"Joe, recognize the man on the window?"

"It's Dino, your number one enemy," Joe said, grabbing Travis's arm. "Let's get out of here."

Travis kept his composure. He looked back at Dino and, without hesitation, said, "He doesn't appear ferocious to me."

"Take my word. People fear him. He's a violent man, and you must avoid provoking him. Dino enjoys throwing blows and won't hesitate to engage in battle."

Travis formed a frown. "If he wants a fight, I must take on the challenge. I'm ready to fight for Pearl's honor and freedom. Dino doesn't intimidate me."

Dino pushed open the window and called out from the balcony.

With a raspy voice and a thick Italian accent, he said. "Hey, you, come on up here. I want to make a business proposition with you."

Travis appeared skeptical but fixed his eyes on Dino. His eyebrows rose, and in a deep voice, he asked. "You want to make a business proposition with me?"

"See anyone else standing around loafing?" Dino asked.

A smile crossed Travis's face. "I'll be right there."

"Travis, don't make it easy for this man to grill you. It's obvious he's aware of your relationship with Pearl."

"Yes, I've considered that someone has informed him of our meeting in secret."

Travis gave his friend a self-assured glance, hoping to relax him. "The old man doesn't intimidate me."

"Because he's old and small in stature, which doesn't mean he's not packing a gun. You must stay alert."

Travis glanced up at the balcony. Dino had disappeared out of view.

"You must make sure Pearl's still alive. It allows me to assess the place for a rescue."

Joe sighed and took to the stairs after Travis.

"No," Travis said, stretching his hand to stop Joe

from following him. "I must go alone. I insist."

"This is a strange scenario," Joe said. "They must be members of the Mafia before a Mafioso hires them. Death to those who get in their way, it's how they understand their beliefs. But I understand your circumstances. Do what you consider best."

I can't involve Joe in this scenario, Travis thought.

The idea of Joe getting hurt is out of the question.

As Travis ascended the stairs, a glint of sunlight peeked through the clouds and blinded him. For a second, he lost traction and came close to falling. With a quick reaction, he caught his balance.

"Consider it a warning," Joe said. "Don't fall for Dino's lies. Adhere to common sense. Watch your step and your back and prepare for trouble."

"Don't worry," Travis assured his friend. "I'll find out what's on Dino's mind."

When Travis reached the top of the stairs, the door opened. A short man stood in front of him. "Come in," he said, gesturing for Travis to follow him.

Travis moseyed along behind the man. He led him through a hallway and into Dino's office. Travis's attention was drawn to a rifle leaning against the wall of the corridor on a set of deer antlers.

"What a handsome rifle," he said. "Who's the hunter here?"

"No, hunter," the servant said. "Dino paid top dollar for the little treasure."

In Dino's office, Travis saw large, oversized chairs and an enormous bearskin rug on the hardwood floor. Everything was larger than normal.

The room emitted a distinctive odor—the smell of a giant ashtray or a musty fog—which caused him to stifle a cough. From behind a desk came a cloud of smoke. Travis missed the aroma of a sweet cigar.

When the smoke cleared, Travis noticed Dino

behind the puff of smoke. Dino had lit an enormous cigar. Travis saw a significant fresh slash across Dino's forehead.

Ah, it's a giveaway sign of malicious behavior, Travis thought.

"What a nasty gash on your forehead. Did you have an accident?" Travis asked.

"Oh, it's a small rip," Dino said.

Travis assumed this came from the accident intended to end his and Pearl's lives. Dino will never admit to being the one trying to kill them.

Dino's cigar flared to life. He smiled and said, "Welcome to my casa. Try one of my cigars," he handed Travis the cigar.

"No, thanks," Travis replied. "Never indulge in smoking" Travis remained edgy and watchful.

"Fine," Dino said, squashing the cigar in a vast ashtray. He rose from his oversized leather chair and extended his hand to shake Travis's hand. He asked, "Lei capisce Italiano?"

Travis nodded and replied, "Capire Italiano un po."

"I'll use ingles on you," Dino said.

"Grazie," Travis said.

"Nonc'è di che," Dino said.

"To keep our conversation tidy, we must use English," Travis said.

"Or avoid trouble," Dino said, chuckling.

"Where did you learn to speak English?" Travis asked.

"I'm a traveling man, and my business is learning languages whenever possible. I'm a well-informed man."

Dino paused a moment, gazed at Travis with intensity, and added, "I've kept my eye on you."

"And what's the reason for staying engaged in my business?"

"You're restless and in need of a job. It'll keep you busy and out of trouble."

"Wrong, I have plenty to carry out."

"I'm offering you a job!" Dino replied in a scornful tone.

Travis remained baffled but gave him his full attention.

Dino continued with his proposal. "I need a driver. Interested in a job as my chauffeur?" he asked with a smile.

"No, thanks, not interested."

"I have another position you're perfect for," he said, awaiting his response.

"Pearl, my girlfriend needs protection when I'm away."

Dino's offer surprised him, but Travis struggled to relax.

"Who's Pearl?" he asked.

Dino's demeanor changed. "Oh, come now, everybody knows Pearl, and I know you're acquainted with her."

"It's obvious I'm on your mind much of the time," Travis said.

Dino smiled and raised his hand, using a gesture to dismiss the statement.

"Have you considered hiring one of your men as a bodyguard?"

"Look here, my young friend. Please appreciate what I'm offering you. It doesn't include a full-time job. I'll need you part-time. Pearl has a permanent bodyguard. She's my Donna, and I need to know she's in expert hands when I'm away.

"You must make sure the grounds stay trouble-free from anyone who comes to buy drugs."

What does Dino have in mind? Travis thought. He's not concerned about giving two lovers a chance to escape from this dungeon. Why give us the opportunity? Days ago, he took on a mission to kill us. Now he wants to hire me to protect Pearl. What's on your mind, Mister?

Travis stayed silent but rejoiced in knowing Pearl had survived the ordeal.

"Well, what's the problem?" Dino asked when Travis didn't answer.

"No problem," Travis said, trying his best not to show emotion.

Dino smiled. "So, tell me, will you agree to guard my women?"

"I'll consider it a privilege."

Pearl remained in Travis's mind as his primary concern. He refused to add fuel to the fire by admitting she was the reason for his visit.

Dino's eyes narrowed, and he said, "What are you doing in this neighborhood?"

"Getting acquainted with Italy."

"Fine," Dino said. "but let me warn you," He moseyed back to his desk, placed his elbows on the desktop, and gave Travis a staring look. "Pearl sei mi numero uno en mi casa," he said, "sei mi fidanzata."

"If she's your fiancée, why does she need guarding?" Travis asked, keeping his tone flat.

"We've discussed getting married. I'm reluctant because Pearl enjoys sitting in the driver's seat."

Travis smiled with affection when Pearl strolled into the room. She looked fragile and broken. I'll apply myself to the fullest in this job to avoid her fears. Pearl will survive, he thought.

Pearl gave Travis a brief look and lowered her eyes.

The tension in the room was intense able. Pearl's blush betrayed her embarrassment, caught between two strong-willed men. Travis, with his towering presence, stood up for her, condemning Dino's disrespectful behavior. The air crackled with anticipation as Dino glared back at Travis, his anger simmering. It was a standoff, and everyone knew it could escalate at any moment.

Dino pulled her as you do a dog on a leash.

Agony penetrated Travis's heart. Dino glared at him but continued his roughness with Pearl.

Pearl didn't honor Dino in Travis's presence, which angered Dino. He grabbed her arm, squeezed, and used foul language.

Travis condemned the words Dino used on Pearl. He found Dino's actions unforgivable.

"Treating a woman with disrespect is despicable."

"This doesn't concern you," Dino said.

"A lack of proper respect for a woman is my concern."

Travis paused and awaited Dino's reaction. He expected the incident to get intense at any moment.

Dino glared at Travis when he surprised him with his outburst. "Stay out of this, or you'll answer to my men!" Dino said.

As they faced off, the room seemed to shrink around them. Travis's resolve was unyielding, and Dino's threats only fueled the fire. The clash of wills was like a storm gathering strength, and the outcome remained uncertain. But Travis knew this battle was worth fighting, even if he risked everything. And in that charged moment, he stood firm, ready to face whatever consequences came his way. The room held its breath, waiting for the storm to break.

Travis and Dino stared at each other. Neither one appeared ready to admit defeat.

A smile crossed Dino's lips. "You're right." Dino turned to Pearl, saying, "We'll resolve this at another time." Dino pointed to a low, silk-cushioned ottoman. "Have a seat," he said. "This will take a minute."

Dino pulled Pearl's arm with a forceful yank and escorted her to another room.

Travis heard a door slam.

"I must use self-control. Lord, I'm sorry I may have created more trouble for Pearl."

Travis strolled over to a window, pulled back the heavy drapes, and flooded the room with light. He noticed a disturbing scene. Four windows bolted shut. What a despicable man, he thought. I assume Dino bolted every window in the house to protect any rescue or escape. I'm overwhelmed by such a finding. I suppose I'll never be able to rescue Pearl from this place.

Travis collapsed in a chair and mulled over the whole scenario. His face looked anguished, etched with pain.

Dino's the boorish enemy after me. He wants to taunt me before he kills me. To trust him is foolish. I know what he plans for me.

When Dino returned, three prominent gangsters followed him.

Two goons grabbed a chair without a nod toward Travis's way. Pearl's bodyguard gave a nod of acknowledgment.

"I learned you've stumbled upon two of my men in their worst behavior. I'm sorry for the confusion," Dino said, and pointed to the brawniest gangster. "Gino's my main butt and enforcer. In gunfights, he's unstoppable and will use any force needed to finish his mission."

"Gino," Dino said, "meet our newest member."

Travis nodded. "Yes, I remember him."

Gino sat on the overstuffed chair the entire time, stone-faced.

He's the belligerent one, Travis considered.

Gino glanced in Travis's direction but didn't greet him.

Dino introduced the second goon. "And Jim is my capo. He's unpredictable but an influential member and excellent with firearms."

"Yes, I remember the one who thumped me. Did you call it confusion? Hard to accept.

It's more of an aggressive attack on a defenseless

person."

Jim stepped forward as if to challenge Travis.

"Mistaken identity, I apologize," Dino said.

Jim stared at Travis the whole time and appeared ready for an altercation.

Jim is the surliest and most belligerent man I've ever met. Travis thought.

"And last but not least, Frankie, Pearl's bodyguard," Dino said. "He's an ambitious person, and even with his large build, he moves with silent speed. He's a self-reliant and resourceful man."

"Men, welcome Travis into the group," Dino said with a grin.

Frankie stepped forward, extended his colossal hand, and gave Travis a quick handshake.

Frankie's brow furrowed. "You look familiar. Have we met?"

Travis smiled and shrugged.

Yes, I remember you, Travis thought. You're the henchman who strolled alongside Pearl the day I met her. You waited outside the entrance while Pearl and I engaged in conversation.

After the introduction, Dino dismissed his men.

~*~*~*~

After his men left, a smile crossed Dino's face, and he said, "You've met my most trusted men. You'll meet others as the opportunity arises. Did you see the men on the rooftop and in the yard? They're my men," he said with a grin as if to intimidate Travis.

His ego may have driven him to express himself in a reputable way.

"This job requires having someone to protect Pearl. Here's where you come in, and Frankie can help us on the road."

Dino took two steps to shake Travis's hand. "From here on, I'll consider you, my property. I ask no questions and answer zip, which means you must abide by my rules. Get it, my friend?" He said it in a disrespectful tone.

Travis rejected Dino's ownership idea but allowed him to pump his hand.

This handshake refused to offer friendship. One must beware of the handshake of a fraudulent friend.

Dino said in a firm, husky tone, "In this town, we don't have to sign papers to know our responsibilities. I've hired you without a recommendation. Don't you dare cross me?"

Dino paused and threatened Travis again. "I must warn you, Pearl's mine. Don't forget."

Travis kept silent as Dino continued to give him orders.

"Report back tomorrow around nine. We'll take a drive around the city. Don't invite your friend. You get it?"

"Why go for a drive?" Travis asked.

Dino walked to the window and said, "Oh, the answer's simple.

Let's say this village has big ears and mouths."

Surprised at his answer, Travis nodded in confusion.

Dino strolled to his desk and pulled out a small revolver. "I want you to have this. You'll need a weapon if you work for me. Come tomorrow morning for training. Don't disappoint me."

Travis held the gun in his hand and looked surprised. "He handled the gun and said I have no use for a weapon.

"Put the gun away. I loaded it before you came."

Travis did not answer but stuck the gun in his pocket. The short man ushered him to the front door.

There's a saying: keep your friends close, but your enemies closer.

Travis joined Joe, and they hurried along in silence. Pearl remained in his mind.

I must not mention the pistol to Joe. He'll go crazy. But why entrust me with a weapon? Does Dino care about his security? Could he be testing me or want to prove he's courageous and doesn't fear me? He wants me to use it on him. It could be a setup.

He plans my demise, hoping the authorities will judge my end as suicide. And he wants my death to look like it came from this pistol.

Dino may not kill me because the police closely watch him. But he has men who will.

When they'd wandered out of the neighborhood, Travis told Joe, "Pearl's alive. I saw her, but her life hangs by a string."

"What's going on?" Joe asked.

"Dino's control over Pearl is appalling. She will not try to escape. Dino bolted shut the windows in his estate.

"Men fail on their mission to help these girls because Dino's estate is a dungeon. Dino sealed it off from the world.

"Without Pearl's cooperation, I'll fail. God knows I'm unable to help her. But I prefer dying to living without her."

"Joe warned me, "If you venture into his estate, you'll be ensnared, just like the countless others who fell into his traps."

"Dino hired me as a part-time bodyguard for Pearl. He demanded

I will meet with him tomorrow. I have no intention of honoring his order. And, as far as the job goes, It tempts me to accept it for Pearl's sake, but I know my demise awaits me."

"Yeah, Dino's a spiteful man," Joe said. "It's the reason my warnings come often.

"I wanted to beat Dino to a pulp and walk out with Pearl. I backed away when Dino brought in his three giant goons.

These goons surprised me with an attack weeks ago.

To make matters worse, I may have aggravated the situation with Dino and Pearl further by provoking Dino."

"Thank God you're out of there in one piece," Joe said. "Dino gives everyone anxiety in this town."

"He assumes he's a celebrity, but he's a dishonest and dangerous person," Travis said. "Dino's infatuated with Pearl. He finds her irresistible, which makes him more destructive."

"Dino's a womanizer."

Joe agreed.

"Dino's estate reminds me of a fortress. It's hard to imagine trying to free Pearl. But he's duped himself into believing Pearl will marry him."

"Marry him?" Joe asked.

"He considers Pearl his fiancée. Dino mentioned marriage to deter my interest in her. But Pearl's smart and will not devalue or lower herself to Dino's level."

The two young men lapsed into silence. Minutes later, Travis broke the silence and said. "From the moment Dino laid eyes on Pearl, this man has terrorized her. Pearl has no power over her life, and he refuses to release her."

"I get it," Joe said. "Other girls have tried to report him to the local authorities for his activities, but to no avail. These girls' intentions give him a perfect excuse to deny their release. A tactic these gangsters use to control young girls."

"Pearl's a young girl with a tragic history. It's hard to imagine the anguish she's gone through. And there's a matter which leaves me baffled. Dino assigned Pearl a bodyguard. He manages the rest of the girls without a guard."

"Oh, yes, Dino has guards for them too, but Pearl's special to Dino and the rest of the girls might not be here the following week. Dino plans to keep Pearl. These men will move the girls to another country if they become a threat. A place where these girls aren't familiar with the region or language."

Travis hung his head and kept his stride while listening to Joe.

"Dino's saving Pearl her for himself. A rival's fight for control can destroy everyone involved.

People might go crazy when they lose the person, they care for the most. Dino, the rival you're addressing, is a significant and dangerous problem. Dino's a lethal force," Travis said.

"Yes, he's an influential person, and he'll win. Dino knows Pearl's heart belongs to you, which makes him delusional. You don't have the power to neutralize the conflict arising in this struggle for Pearl. Best prepared."

"Do you mean I must leave Pearl behind with Dino? How do you say goodbye to the one you hold dearest in your heart? I have the finances to help her, but I lack a strategy to get her out of Genoa."

"To make a rational decision when you're committed to one person is difficult," Joe said. "You're in a heap of trouble, my friend. You deserve more and must strive to save yourself first."

"I'll strive to save Pearl," he said with annoyance.

"You'll lose the battle. To rescue Pearl is impossible."

They sat on a large boulder overlooking the bay when they reached the yacht.

"I've thought of turning Dino over to the Italian authorities. But I'm afraid Pearl's life will have a vicious ending. The minute Dino learns the Genoese police pursue him because I turned him in, he'll have Pearl killed."

Travis and Joe stayed silent until Travis broke the silence.

"Joe," he said, "imagine reading the headlines of a newspaper saying a homicide has taken two lives."

"Imagine reading the headline, Local Woman Killed.

This report is the police's description of the homicide after receiving a criminal report involving the notorious Dino Carino. Pearl Moreno lost her life last night.

An American man, Travis, tried to rescue Ms. Moreno from Dino's estate, where Dino detained her. Dino's men shot them to death. The investigation is ongoing."

"You've heard what may happen. What do you think?" Travis said.

"This may happen with Dino's state of mind," Joe said.

"The time isn't right now. I must wait and keep a low profile until I have a stable plan," Travis said.

Travis didn't recognize the intense storm before him. His loyalty to Pearl had set the course for constant peril.

CHAPTER 7~THE GOODBYE

Travis dined at one of his favorite restaurants, Zeffirino's, where the staff was zealous and attentive. Zeffirino's history started in 1939, when Zeffirino Belloni opened his restaurant in Genoa.

Travis went alone to compare the restaurant to the one he hoped to manage someday. The food is classic, with fresh Italian ingredients, he thought. If you're ethnic Italian, the taste may appeal to most. The place has an old-fashioned style with basic food, and the price of a meal may need adjusting.

His dream of opening his restaurant continued to fill his thoughts. Finishing The School of Fine Arts of Food is a prerequisite for entry into this profession.

The server approached him. "I'll have grilled calamari and shrimp, my favorite Italian dish," he told the waiter. After he'd ordered, he looked around to get ideas on how to decorate his restaurant. He spotted Pearl and Frankie, her bodyguard. Frankie found a hair in his meal and complained to the chef. It gave Travis ample time to talk to Pearl.

Travis approached Pearl and captured her lips for a second. "Ready for the great escape?" he asked. "It's the perfect time to cut loose from your bodyguard. He's capable of eating alone."

Pearl smiled. "So glad to see you," she said.

"To accept your challenge will be a risky move, but I'm ready. I haven't seen Dino and his men for days.

Frankie will greet each worker in the kitchen and take his time. After which, he'll concentrate on business and complain to the chef."

"I'll contact a taxi, and he'll take us to Florence."

As they made their way out, Travis explained his plans to Pearl. He noticed her eyes fixed on the entrance. A low grumble came from within Pearl.

"What's wrong?" He asked.

"Dino and his date," she said, motioning toward the door.

"We'll wait for the Host to sit them down before we move."

Dino stood with his arm wrapped around his girlfriend's waist, giving her one compliment after another.

"He's such a phony. He plays the part of a perfect gentleman in public, polite and respectable," Pearl said. "The public knows his reputation."

"Honey, forget Dino."

"If we go out, he'll spot us," she said.

"Dino makes everyone aware of his presence, but always at the wrong time. He has a powerful influence on people, called fear."

Extreme dislike for this man consumed Pearl. Her temper kept rising. "I want to slap the smug look off his face."

Travis wanted Pearl to focus on their plan. "Honey," he said, "go out the front. I'll go out the back. The surroundings will camouflage us."

"Travis, I'm scared. Dino's men follow him wherever he goes. I guarantee you; his men have surrounded this place.

"Take my word. Dino's men are under immense pressure. And if they don't give Dino the information he wants, he'll kill them. The free drugs he gives them as payment help keep them in line."

"Honey, concentrate. Let's wait here for a while.

You sneak out when Dino and his date get busy ordering."

"Okay," she said. The fear of imminent danger made her tense.

"Pearl, go," Travis said in a whisper.

"I'll wait until you're out before I leave." Travis pushed her toward the door.

When Pearl delayed showing up, Travis feared something had gone wrong. But Pearl appeared seconds after his fretful moment.

"Dino's men notified him when I arrived here," she said. "The minute I stepped outside, I heard footsteps and my name. Dino asked me if I'd lost my way.

"I told him I needed fresh air. He warned me," he said, "I know he's around here someplace. My men warned me, so I came to see for myself. If I catch you with him, I'll kill you both on the spot."

"The thought of ending our relationship saddens me, but we must go our separate ways. I'm sorry. I love you and thank you for your efforts to rescue me."

Travis saw the hurt in her eyes. "Honey, I've arranged an escape. We must go through the plan today."

Pearl hugged him and gave him a last kiss. "Preparations will take us a short distance," she said. "It's irresponsible to continue in this relationship, which might destroy us. I don't deserve freedom.

"There's no hope left. Fear paralyzes me every time we try to escape. I can't take it anymore. But know this: my heart belongs to you."

A grunt escaped from Travis's lips. "This can't happen. Please take a leap of faith. Without faith, we're at a disadvantage."

Travis held his head in his hands. I must convince her that my way is not dangerous, he thought.

He sensed her fear and dismay, but he considered himself defeated. "I love you," he whispered.

Pearl stared into Travis's cloudy eyes.

"Yes, I know," she said. "You've captured my heart, too. But my life's in turmoil. I must go back and meet Frankie before Dino finds me with you. He'll kill us on the spot."

"We'll call the police authorities. They'll protect us on the way to the airport."

"The law won't help us sneak someone out of the country's illegal. And there're consequences for sneaking into another country."

"We'll go for a visit to a neighboring city and lie low."

"Dino has contacts inside the police department. There're men I haven't met."

Travis held her hand and said, "Please, listen to me."

She paused for a moment and then forced her hand away from his grip. Travis stared at Pearl as she walked back to danger. The outcome did not meet his expectations.

~*~*~*~

Late afternoon, Travis met Joe at The Walk-In Café.

"I saw Pearl today at Zeffirinos," Travis said, his voice tinged with a mix of sadness and longing.

"Yeah," Joe said."

"Have you any remedies for healing a broken heart after a wrecked relationship?"

Joe wrinkled his brows and peeked over his sunglasses. "I hear you loud and clear. Pearl ended the relationship, right?" he asked. he asked.

"Yes, I didn't convince her. Her fear is profound."

"Travis, she'll manage without you. Your love for her prevents you from seeing the danger of your relationship."

He ignored Joe and rested his gaze on a mountaintop in the distance, its jagged peaks piercing the sky. These mountains, rugged and untamed, remind me of Pearl.

Travis removed his cap and scratched his head. Pearl considers there's something mysterious in a mountain that creates joy and fear simultaneously, a bittersweet sentiment.

"Mountains cause different emotions for everyone," Joe said.

With his face contorted in anguish, Travis's voice trembled as he said, "Lord, I must find a way to convince Pearl to trust me."

"I'm concerned about what may happen to Pearl after I leave."

Joe sighed and said, "A Day of déjà vu again. Men have expressed the same concern for these young women at various times, but Dino has killed them. Protect yourself against heroism. Dino's a powerful tyrant and one to fear.

"Mothers tell children, keep away from Dino. Travis, you must do the same."

"What can we do?" Travis asked.

Joe shrugged.

"Pearl mentioned Dino's a jealous man," Travis said. "He refuses to surrender his pride and joy."

"Let me give you the facts about the mafia. Young children become attracted to this organization. Once they join, they seldom leave. But the mafia reacts coldly when a new member makes a mistake."

"You mean they kill them?"

"Right, this organization is as vicious as a snake. Money makes them proud and takes priority over a commitment to a woman or a child. And the mob seldom includes anyone outside a family circle in Dino's job offers to you, which surprised me. He wants to win your trust but will turn on you."

Travis nodded, "I know Dino used Pearl to entrap me," he said, shrugging.

"My friend, you've stepped into a mine about to explode," Joe said with a deep, worrisome look.

"I have no choice. Pearl needs my help." He drew his brows close and spread his arms out. "What else can I do?"

"Let me tell you what the mafia stands for," Joe said. "These vast organizations span continents, trade what's illegal, and have endless connections.

"Corruption is still a significant problem in Italy. Companies, shopkeepers, and craft workers must pay protection money to crime syndicates. The mafia controls neighborhoods, and people fear these criminals."

Joe continued. "And there're various groups. Yes, groups in Italy alone. But they spread across the entire globe. There's an intelligent way to stay alive, and Pearl will survive your recklessness if you walk away and forget your rescue. Go home, Travis."

"There's one way you'll convince me to go home."

"What a disturbing thought. Whenever I give you my opinion on taking a different path, you amaze me with the same pitiful ideas. Your attention span is limited. Your crazy idea will never work."

"You've taken Dino's side," Travis said, swallowed the last sip of his soda, and wandered away. Joe had dented his intelligence.

~*~*~*~

A breath of fresh air will invigorate me. And I know Joe speaks the truth. I must go back to America without Pearl.

After Joe rebuked Travis, Pearl ended their relationship. He was alone and friendless in a distant land.

Travis's birthday will arrive in days, but he refuses to celebrate with Joe. His pessimistic outlook toward Pearl annoyed him.

I grew restless and homesick. Thoughts of America crossed my mind. "A quick visit with relatives and friends will enhance my life. I'm eager to see them," he whispered. "I must call Mrs. Ellen and ask for an extended leave of absence."

This gun Dino gifted me with has become a liability. It would be best if I hid his weapon in a safe place. For sure, I can't carry a concealed handgun in my luggage. The history of this gun worries me. Dino might want to pin a murder on me or intend it for unknown purposes.

I'll hide this firearm on the yacht and handle the problem when I return from America. He convinced himself he must go to America to check on his house. The real reason showed on his face: loneliness.

~*~*~*~

Back home, three of his friends settled in Travis's recreation room.

Monday night, football came on his birthday. They watched the Denver Broncos go against the Oakland Raiders at Mile High Stadium.

I'm pleased to have celebrated my birthday with my best friends and to cheer for our favorite team.

Visiting relatives and friends in my old neighborhood gives me immense joy. Playing football and hanging out will make way for losing all my belongings, but football games with friends helped me look at life from my father's perspective.

Travis needed a job. He missed his father, who left responsibility and decisions on his shoulders.

While deciding whether to continue school or quit, I'll work on this property and prepare the lawn for the summer. Dad kept this lawn well-manicured. I consider yard work an enormous task, like a permanent job, or counting stars in the sky. But I know it's a well-deserved reward received at the end.

Travis stayed busy, worked hard, and refused to allow his thoughts to travel to Genoa. His work time bled into his rest time.

His father's desk became number one for separating items he wanted to keep.

"What an impressive desk," his chum said. "The mahogany still looks new. Can I persuade you to sell this desk?" his friend asked.

"No, it has too much sentimental value."

Travis raised a portrait of his father. His friend commented with kindness and respect. "Yes, Malcolm Steele proved himself a man of dignity and deserved recognition. I know you've missed him."

"The two items I hold dear, his desk and his portrait. I lived a sweet and serene life with Dad. He raised me with morals, and I escaped a life of crime."

A nod came from his friend. "Mr. Steele kept a tight rein on you, and now you're a respected man in this neighborhood."

Travis nodded. "Thank you."

"Life's a journey, and Dad was my hero. He taught me by example to respect others, work hard under pressure, and have confidence. I've learned these skills when adversities in life occur. It would be best if you did not let them control you. And Dad taught me how to conquer fear by gazing into terror with firmness."

A pause. "I know my father's old restaurant still stands. I'd want to know if his past customers still patronize the place?" Travis asked.

"Yes, it's one of my favorite places to eat. We must have dinner there tonight?"

Travis smiled and nodded.

When Travis entered his father's old restaurant, he smiled with delight. His dream of opening an Italian Bistro still existed deep in his soul.

Travis was resolute as he called Ms. Ellen in Genoa. "Please assure me the class has not started, and is it possible for me to return to Genoa and complete my education?"

"Yes, you must return. We are a month away from orientation. A small warning: you will face hot summers in

Italy, even in the northern regions.

"Italians take August off. There's a mass exodus to beaches and mountains to find a cool breeze and a shady place. Wait a couple of weeks.

"Living the lifestyle of a beach drifter's a dream," he said.

"But can't earn a living daydreaming."

Travis refused to spend more time in Genoa than necessary. Without Pearl, he'd lost his appetite for the beach.

~*~*~*~

Three weeks later, Travis started planning his return to Genoa. Six months left of this uphill struggle in school, he thought. I must call Joe and let him know. I hope his yacht's available to rent. To return to Genoa makes me uncomfortable, but I must face whatever awaits me.

Months after, Travis did what he'd returned for in Genoa.

"My last day of school has arrived, which allows me the freedom to travel back home or stay in Italy. I've topped the class and won the honor of having my name attached to the roster of chefs. This honor has allowed me to join the big guys. I'll have to get my name known," he whispered.

Travis looked forward to starting his venture into the restaurant business but needed a partner. He knew of one qualified man, his friend Joe.

Travis asked Joe, "Does the restaurant business still interest you? Come to America and help me run a restaurant."

Joe glanced at Travis and gave him a puzzled look but came short of giving him an answer.

"Let me know when I return," Travis said, leaving like a whirlwind. He was on a mission.

When I returned to Genoa, Pearl captured my thoughts the entire time. Before returning home, I'll visit

Dino and plead for Pearl. Denying her may cause an altercation or my demise.

"Dear God," Travis said, "If I cannot free Pearl this time, I'll accept it as the will of my Lord. I've done everything in my power to rescue her."

When I arrived at Dino's neighborhood, I looked around for his intimidators. I questioned if any of them had situated themselves with guns drawn. They hang around and await intruders to show their faces and shoot them. Dino provides them with free drugs."

Travis wiped his sweaty palms off his pants and knocked.

Someone called out for me to enter. As I entered, I heard a gunshot. And I ducked and fell, landing in the entryway with a thud.

The scene startled me. My heartbeat was fast, carrying a drum tune. A rifle hung from the ceiling, and Dino appeared strapped to a chair.

"What's going on here?" I asked.

I tried to make sense of the scenery before me.

Seeing Dino's feet inches from where I fell, saddled to a chair, a rope going in every direction, gripped my soul. What a troubling scene.

I remember seeing this rifle hanging in Dino's hallway.

People own rifles to hunt, admire, or consider an heirloom. To use a gun another way demands extreme care by a sane person.

"Who fired the shot?" Travis asked as he struggled to stand.

Dino has lived a contemporary life, but now he looks like a wild man, Travis thought. Accepting his outward show is hard, and his hygiene emits an unpleasant odor. His dirty clothes degrade him. Travis conceived its neglect of essential cleanliness and a dull moment in Dino's life.

Travis's eyes shifted to the ceiling. "What's the contraption intended for?" Travis asked. Dino remained silent, but his glance up at the rifle gave Travis the answer to Dino's intent.

"As I understand this death trap, when I opened the door, the rope tied to the handle pulled the trigger, which caused the rifle to fire. Right?"

"The bullet missed its target, my head," Dino said and sighed.

"God forbid," Travis said. "Why," He asked. "Why do you want to commit suicide?"

"Don't stand there gawking. Untie me!"

Travis ignored his plea.

"Untie me or get out," Dino said.

Travis struggled to find his voice and glanced around for his men, but none showed their faces.

"What happened to your bodyguard?"

"Why should it concern you?"

Travis stared at the Mafioso, who remained strapped to the chair with no bargaining power. With little to lose or fear, he briefed Dino on what he expected on this visit.

"I don't care why this happened, but I've come for Pearl."

Dino glanced at Travis and said. "Don't you know?"

A frown formed on Travis's forehead. "What have you done to Pearl?"

"You'll never comprehend," Dino said.

"Tell me before I get it out of you."

"Okay, I'll fill you in on what happened." Dino paused.

"Go on, Travis said." He glanced around the room before giving Dino his full attention.

Pearl went to sea, left on my boat, and has yet to return.

Travis screamed while squinting and tilting his head. His voice got louder. You're lying.

"My boat was found capsized by the Coast Guard. For days, the police helped in the search. They believed she fell overboard. They found no trace of Pearl."

Travis's complexion grew pallid. Travis grabbed Dino's shirt collar. "I want to shoot you with your rifle, but it would be too simple. You are a man of dishonesty! Please explain what you did to her."

Travis punched him twice, and Dino went silent.

Travis punched him twice, and Dino went silent.

"No! No! No!" he screamed. "Lord, it's as if someone ripped out my heart." Travis wept.

Dino mumbled his words. "The men have abandoned me because the authorities found someone dead in my basement. They think I murdered him. But I know the girls killed him and fled the premises."

"What makes you think I care? I'm glad the girls gained their freedom."

After minutes had passed, Dino said. "These girls will report me to the authorities, and the polizia will come after me, but they must kill me before they take me away. I will not give them any information."

Travis shook his head in disbelief. "What a narcissist," Travis said.

"Pearl, what made you go out alone? Who drove you to this desperation?" he cried out. "Oh, Pearl, I'm sorry I left you to fight your own battle."

Travis stood in front of the enormous window overlooking the neighborhood. He bowed his head and clenched his hands around the drapes.

He turned to Dino and said. "You allowed her to go out on the boat alone?"

"I brought my boat from Florence to have it serviced. Pearl sneaked the boat past Frankie. He informed me of the accident when I returned from a business trip. I'm alone with no one to care for me."

"This must've happened in recent days?"

"It happened back in August."

Travis strolled over to the window and stared out into space. His teeth clenched tight, and his hands balled into fists. "Lord, please help me. I'm afraid I'll lose control, go into a wild rage, and hurt this man," he whispered.

Sorrow triggered a powerful emotion. Travis buried his face on the edge of the drapes and wept.

"Lord, help me comprehend Pearl's mysterious disappearance." Travis's fingers dug into the palm of his hands. And he prayed under his breath. Lord, you allowed this mysterious tragedy to happen. Pearl meant everything to me. Please help me cope with this loss.

Confusion causes fear, which keeps you from being able to face your past.

Rage flared, and his fingers clamped into fists. Travis punched the wall over and over until his knuckles bled. "I should've used force to remove Pearl from this place."

"Lord, how can this fit into your plan?" Travis's tears rolled. "I need to hear her voice, to see her face. Pearl's death will be mine."

Without a word, Travis turned and faced the pitiful man, still saddled in the chair, his chin on his chest. "You said you banned her from going anywhere alone."

"No, not true. I allowed Pearl to venture. I promised to keep her safe and give her what she needed. Pearl returned home because loyalty brought her back."

"Dino, you live in a fantasy world. Why can't you tell the truth? You deprived her of coming and going as she pleased. Don't tarnish her memory with lies."

Dino's chin rested on his chest. Eyes cast to the floor. In a raspy voice, he said, "Io parlai la verit."

Travis stared at Dino. "You're a deceitful man." Travis turned around to leave, but Dino pleaded with him. "Please untie me. I don't know when someone will come to visit me. I paid someone to tie me up with no intention of changing my mind. But my rifle misfired."

"Pearl lived miserable under your rule, and you tried to kill us. And now you want me to help you? How can I help someone so extreme and dangerous?"

Travis marched back in with the handgun Dino had given him.

"Go ahead, shoot me," Dino said. "I've lost my love. I may as well die."

"You've become a danger to every man. It's best if you cease to exist. I won't rescue you from your misery. Here's your gun. I have no use for a weapon." Travis said and placed the gun on the table.

"It's a gift from me."

Travis hurried out.

Dino kicked and screamed, "Don't leave me this way! I beg of you!"

As I stepped out the door, I experienced a slight breeze and imagined Dino tied to the chair. I stopped, my body folded in a crouched position and my head bowed. God tells me His way differs from mine.

Travis had experienced a spiritual moment.

"Lord, give me the willpower to help this man. If I leave Dino in this position, he'll die. To find healing, I must forgive and value the life of my enemy. I must have sympathy for your sake and glory," he prayed.

"Lord, Dino has destroyed lives, but today, I met a man who needs help. You sent me here, Lord. And I'm compelled to impart my limited knowledge of your word to this man.

"Strengthen me, Lord. With Pearl gone, there's no threat toward one another anymore." Travis went back to untie and talked to Dino. Desperate to free himself, his chair had tumbled over, sending Dino to the floorboards, where he lay kissing the floor.

"I returned to encourage you to consider a different

path," Travis said. He turned the chair upright, with Dino still tied to it. Dino hung his head, and when Travis asked if he wanted prayer, the Mafioso declined.

"I attend church. God has blessed me. I'm a good man."

"There's not one soul who can claim he's good," Travis said.

Dino made a facial expression.

"God disapproves of your illicit life. And you can't change His Word to suit whatever deluded and wicked deeds you achieve." Travis said.

"You've heard God; our creator cares for us. God has the power to fulfill any promise He makes."

Travis tried for thirty minutes to enlighten Dino with God's love.

Dino refused to accept his kindness and considered making the will of the Lord and prayer a nuisance.

"The duties and responsibilities you count as a nuisance today might surprise you. It's a part of God's need for our life. A means by which God lifts your soul and prepares it for eternity," Travis said.

Dino responded with a negative comment, and Travis didn't care to reply to his inappropriate comment.

"Enough. I've had it with your 'poor me' approach," Travis said.

Not expecting a change from Dino, Travis turned to leave when he noticed his demeanor softened.

"I'll try to figure it out," Dino said, tears forming.

Encouraged by Dino's unexpected change, Travis prayed with him.

"God will give you knowledge," Travis said.

Dino said he wanted to leave the mafia organization and turn to the Lord for guidance. "Grazie," he said, "Thank you for your help in my darkest hour."

"God's a merciful God," Travis said. "He'll turn whatever you meant for destruction to good, for His glory.

This place brought so much suffering to Pearl and every girl who entered through those doors. The girls wanted to enjoy the freedom and live without being controlled or abused by criminals."

When he finished, he untied Dino and dashed out. He never wanted to see Dino again.

"You've become a danger to every man. It's best if you cease to exist. I won't rescue you from your misery. Here's your gun. I have no use for a weapon." Travis said and placed the gun on the table.

"It's a gift from me."

Travis hurried out.

Dino kicked and screamed, "Don't leave me this way! I beg of you!"

As I stepped out the door, I experienced a slight breeze and imagined Dino tied to the chair. I stopped, my body folded in a crouched position and my head bowed. God tells me His way differs from mine.

Travis had experienced a spiritual moment.

"Lord, give me the willpower to help this man. If I leave Dino in this position, he'll die. To find healing, I must forgive and value the life of my enemy. I must have sympathy for your sake and glory," he prayed.

"Lord, Dino has destroyed lives, but today, I met a man who needs help. You sent me here, Lord. And I'm compelled to impart my limited knowledge of your word to this man.

"Strengthen me, Lord. With Pearl gone, there's no threat toward one another anymore."

Travis went back to untie and talked to Dino. Desperate to free himself, his chair had tumbled over, sending Dino to the floorboards, where he lay kissing the floor.

"I returned to encourage you to consider a different path," Travis said.

He turned the chair upright, with Dino still tied to it.

Dino hung his head, and when Travis asked if he wanted prayer, the Mafioso declined.

"I attend church. God has blessed me. I'm a good man."

"There's not one soul who can claim he's good," Travis said.

Dino made a facial expression.

"God disapproves of your illicit life. And you can't change His Word to suit whatever deluded and wicked deeds you achieve." Travis said.

"You've heard God; our creator cares for us. God has the power to fulfill any promise He makes."

Travis tried for thirty minutes to enlighten Dino with God's love.

Dino refused to accept his kindness and considered making the will of the Lord and prayer a nuisance.

"The duties and responsibilities you count as a nuisance today might surprise you. It's a part of God's need for our life. A means by which God lifts your soul and prepares it for eternity," Travis said.

Dino responded with a negative comment, and Travis didn't care to reply to his inappropriate comment.

"Enough. I've had it with your 'poor me' approach," Travis said.

Not expecting a change from Dino, Travis turned to leave when he noticed his demeanor softened.

"I'll try to figure it out," Dino said, tears forming.

Encouraged by Dino's unexpected change, Travis prayed with him.

"God will give you knowledge," Travis said.

Dino said he wanted to leave the mafia organization and turn to the Lord for guidance. "Grazie," he said,

"Thank you for your help in my darkest hour."

"God's a merciful God," Travis said. "He'll turn whatever you meant for destruction to good, for His glory. This place brought so much suffering to Pearl and every girl who entered through those doors. The girls wanted to enjoy the freedom and live without being controlled or abused by criminals."

When he finished, he untied Dino and dashed out. He never wanted to see Dino again.

~*~*~*~

After leaving Dino's place, Travis wandered to the beach and spent the day with cloudy thoughts. Travis tasted salt on his lips, the ocean water, and tears.

I missed the chance to say goodbye. I'll miss you forever. The nightmare's over, little girl. It hurts to know you're gone. I'll miss you. I'll grieve in silence for the rest of my life for you.

My passion, my inspiration, and my best friend are gone. If it's God's plan, we'll meet again. I'll look at the sky every night and know you're safe. Loving you will remain the sweetest memory I'll ever have. Death takes the body, but God takes the soul.

Travis stared out into the ocean's empty vastness and recalled every feature of Pearl. He missed her blue eyes, delicate facial features, soft voice, and perfect lips.

Travis held himself responsible for Pearl's death. He had promised to rescue her but failed.

I watch people pass by without a nod, which may lighten the deep gloom. Plagued and overwhelmed, I experienced a journey of deep affliction, but no cure appeared for my suffering.

The world goes on, unconcerned, but my life has collapsed. I can't mention my loneliness and sorrow to anyone. They cannot respond because they don't have empathy. When you're disabled on the inside, nothing can make the pain leave, so you must hide it with a smile.

Travis questioned his faith. God, you've allowed this to happen for a reason, but I can't make sense of this in my mind.

Joe saw Travis and sat close to him.

"What brings you here?" Travis asked.

"I'm out on my evening run and spotted my friend looking lonesome."

Travis smiled. "I've spent hours brooding over my future and lost track of time."

"Sounds like a movie. Tell me the conclusion."

"I made my way to Dino's today."

"You don't learn."

Travis sighed and said, "Pearl's gone."

Joe wrote a word on the sand with his finger. "Yes," he said, "it was a terrible accident. I struggled to tell you about her misfortune. And I'm sorry it happened."

Travis turned to face Joe. "I don't understand."

Joe gave him a sorrowful glance and looked away.

"Oh, I get it," Travis said. "How long have you known of her drowning?"

"Same day, the accident occurred."

"You've known for several months and neglected to tell me?"

Travis held his composure, but his anger increased by the minute. "Friends don't wrong friends by withholding valuable information. I told you I wanted to confront Dino about my intentions for Pearl."

"I started to tell you countless times, but the right words escaped me. You've suffered enough trials here in Italy, and adding more misery made little sense."

Joe continued. "I feared you might hurt Dino and do prison time. I recognize that you adored her with your whole heart. But you lacked the power at the time to subdue your situation. And I fear it might disrupt your school.

"You stayed in America for a year, and I hoped your attraction for Pearl no longer existed."

Travis looked away to blink back his tears. "I'm a grown man. I don't need nurturing. You'll never figure me out.

The decision that you made belonged to me." With

his eyes still focused on the sea, he said. "There's nothing worse than to have your best friend mask the truth from you."

"I'm sorry, man."

"This is crushing news; I need a remedy for a shattered heart."

"Please, believe me, I've punished myself enough for not telling you. I knew someday you'd hold me accountable. I gambled you'd appreciate my decision."

Someday I may be grateful you took matters into your own hands."

"Sorry, you feel this way," Joe said.

Here is advice from this friend: cherish the time you spend with friends. Respect and honor their wishes."

The men went silent.

"There's another issue to address. The storm has ended, but life will not have a new beginning without Pearl."

"Yeah, life's hard." Joe replied, "Maybe Dino arranged her death."

"If anyone's responsible for her death, it's me." He fixed his eyes on the sea. "An accident may have happened, but it started with desperation and the loneliness she experienced."

"Given the chaotic circumstances of her demise, I'm sure Dino had something to do with escalating her death. It's a sad time," Joe sighed.

Travis answered Joe's questions but refused to join him in his gloomy chat.

"Listen, Joe," Travis said. "It's difficult to carry on a conversation about Pearl's death. Mind if we change the topic?"

"Sure," Joe said. I hope that someday you'll see it my way.

Travis shook his head and turned to face Joe. "No, it will never happen."

Joe looked stunned.

"When the storm has passed and you've survived, your life has changed," Travis said. "I can't claim my storm's over, but there's one problem. The secret of my storm continues to hold me hostage and wants to cut me to rubble. The person I will become after the typhoon, God only knows."

CHAPTER 8~PARTNERS IN BUSINESS

Genoa, Italy.

In March, the weather in Italy becomes more unpredictable. March weather means rain or dampness, and it's still wintry in other places.

Deeply wounded by Pearl's demise, Travis found himself in desperate need of closure. Amid his mourning, he found it unbearable to face Joe, shutting himself off from his friend's attempts to reach out. Travis battled with his emotions, wrestling with the decision to reconcile with Joe. This decision, a beacon of hope, was a sign that Travis was ready to start healing. After three long, solitary months of mourning, Travis mustered the courage to extend an olive branch, inviting Joe for a lunch meeting.

Joe respected the way Travis managed his grief.

"Pearl once lived in Boccadse, a place that held a special meaning for both of us," Travis said, his voice filled with nostalgia and pain.

"Yes, I remember her as a child when I lived there."

"I have no regrets about meeting and falling in love with Pearl. I wish I'd spent more quality time with her. She lived a tough life. When you run away from home, you must change how you live, but there are times when paranoia decides for you.

"When a person's unable to live in a secure environment, you know someone will hit their target someday, and it'll be over for you. This statement goes for anyone who may influence your emotions and judgments."

"Yes," Joe said. "Distorted perceptions can affect our emotional state and come with pricey consequences."

"The Lord allowed me to explain my faith to Pearl. And when I finished, the rest is history." Travis heaved a sigh.

"I promised Pearl, I'd free her from Dino's clutches." He paused, and a lump in his throat inflicted a searing pain. "Sorry," he said, clearing his throat. "I" failed in my calling, and it keeps eating at me." His unfulfilled promise, a heavy burden, was a constant, nagging reminder of his perceived failure.

"You did your best to keep your promise," Joe said, his voice filled with empathy and understanding. The time spent with Joe became a moment of forgiveness, a significant step towards healing. Travis, in a moment of profound relief, forgave Joe for withholding information about Pearl's death, understanding that Joe had his reasons and his pain to bear.

~*~*~*~

When they returned from lunch at *The Walk-In Café*, Travis, visibly worn out and emotionally spent, found solace on the curb outside Joe's apartment. After what seemed like an eternity, Joe extended an invitation for coffee. Travis didn't respond. He had lived in isolation for three months, detached from the world; his once vibrant spirit is now a mere flicker. He needed time to adapt to find a new norm and find his place in a drastically changed world.

"How does a cup of coffee sound to you?" Joe asked again.

"Come inside. I don't serve out here."

"I want to enjoy the cool breeze for a few minutes."

Even as Travis took steps towards healing, the memory of Pearl stayed a constant presence. Each day, he experienced a new healing, a slow, gradual process he was learning to navigate.

When he entered, Travis noticed Joe's luggage and belongings stacked in a corner.

"It looks as if you're planning a trip?" He asked.

"My belongings have waited a long time for you."

Travis grinned. "So, Joe, does this mean you're ready to join me in the restaurant business? I must warn you, it's not all fun and games. We'll need to hire a financial adviser."

Joe chuckled and said, "No, I'm the one who ought to warn you. I'm good in the kitchen and no other place."

"That's where I'll need you," Travis said, a glimmer of excitement in his eyes. A shared smile illuminated their faces, a testament to the healing and friendship that had blossomed between them.

"When you surrender your apartment, you can share the yacht with me. And guess where you'll sleep."

"The sofa?"

"Travis, have you made plans to return to America and open a restaurant there?"

"Yes, I'm going back."

"Before we leave, I have a question for you," Joe said.

"I'm listening."

"Have you considered the property I showed you months ago? It's a prime location, and I think it could be a great investment for us

"There's nothing to hold my interest in Genoa. I'm going home."

"Okay, It's understandable."

Late in the afternoon, Travis helped Joe move his belongings to the yacht.

~*~*~*~

Days later, when Travis and Joe sat at the kitchen table, they were deep in conversation. "I'm excited about our plans," Travis said. "I've considered two locations for a restaurant. When I went to New York, I learned they were building a new commercial subdivision near my home. I may rent space there.

"But I may buy my father's old restaurant and refurbish the place. The job will be uphill, and I'll drop my funds there. But I've learned my father's faithful customers still frequent the place."

"I'll help with the cost when my boss cuts my first check," Joe said in good humor.

Travis joined him in laughter. "No, thanks, unless you have more than a paycheck? The inheritance had better be enough to cover all the expenses."

"It's an enormous investment."

"This is the biggest leap I've taken. The thrill of starting this venture is indescribable. It's a journey filled with excitement and hope. I'm grateful that we're in this together, Joe. You'll back my ideas; I'll encourage you and we'll both triumph."

Joe smiled. "People have hopes for brilliant achievements. Others make them happen." His words were filled with optimism and confidence, instilling the same in the audience about the potential success of their partnership.

"Dad said we must take a stand for what we believe. If we can't trust ourselves, no one will. I promised my father I'd pursue his zeal as a chef. But I promised myself I'd share God's good news with people. I must achieve both."

"Travis," Joe said. "Don't decide where to open a business until you check out another site I found. Once a popular place, it's now for sale. This eager entrepreneur wants to sell the restaurant at a reasonable price. The owner's tired of the hot weather and plans to retire in Sweden."

Travis's brows arched, and he gave him a look that implied, I'm interested. "Where's this place?" I hope this interests me and has more value than the last property we saw.

"The property waits for you in La Spezia, south of Genoa City and seventeen miles from La Spezia Centrale.

It's a vibrant area with a growing population and a thriving local economy, making it an ideal location for a new restaurant venture."

"I'm familiar with the location—a picturesque place. La Spezia's not a tourist town but has museums and good transport links. Let's drive there and look."

"I'll make a call. The owner boarded the windows and entrances." Joe said. "We'll check and see if the property is worth our time. If you still want to return home after seeing the inside, I'll go without regret.

"Fair enough."

A smile crossed Travis's face when he saw the property. "It's a surfer's paradise, accessible for other entertainment, and a bonus is sitting by the sea. What sets us apart is our unique menu, featuring rare recipes from top chefs, and our commitment to providing a memorable dining experience."

The owner arrived, eager to show the inside of the place. Travis appeared excited as well.

The owner bragged about his building. "Less than two weeks ago, I installed a new roof and paved the parking lot to improve the property. The inside is in mint condition. I lowered the price for a quick sale."

Travis listened to every word this man spoke, and every word came with an incentive. The following weeks were busy for Travis and Joe as they prepared to open. At the end of the week, Travis ordered new booths and tables to please his taste and style, and Joe rearranged the kitchen according to his needs. Travis and Joe have a moral sense of security, knowing God answered their prayers.

"Here's another feature I want to highlight on the menu," Travis said.

"What's wrong with the menu I've created?"

Travis smiled. "I wish to offer a more significant and quintessential choice. Here's a book called Secrets of a Chef, with rare recipes my father owned. There are a couple of pages missing.

"These recipes will make a good menu. Dad owned the last copy available. Most recipes came from top chefs. I want you to integrate these innovative ideas into the menu. It inspires great creativity with mouthwatering dishes. Make these recipes a priority."

The day after, Travis and Joe met at the restaurant. They discussed making their eating place a prestigious restaurant.

"Thirty-five years ago, a restaurant stood for a place to eat. And twenty years ago, the name chef mattered little. Today, people want to associate with them while they eat their food.

"Today, I'll show you how you can depend on returning customers. Great coffee is important and goes with any meal; it's the kind of coffee you grind before you prepare. Prep time's no hassle. The complex flavors of the beans waft as you take the first perfect sip. I enjoy the entire ritual."

Travis dropped into a chair while Joe poured him a cup of coffee. It's the best coffee in the world, according to Joe.

"I'll have one cup. I drink more coffee than I should."

"Joe winked and slid into a chair. He poured himself a cup and set a pitcher of coffee in front of Travis.

"Joe winked and slid into a chair. He poured himself a cup and set a pitcher of coffee in front of Travis. Joe studied Travis for ten seconds before he swallowed a sip of coffee.

"Help yourself if you change your mind."

Travis took the last sip of his coffee and savored the flavor. Before long, he had poured himself another cup.

"This coffee's excellent. I'd return to this place for the coffee," he said.

"And so will your customers," Joe said. "I roasted

this coffee for this occasion."

"I agree. We need to serve this coffee. Please order a roaster and a grinder."

"I own them both," Joe said.

The conversation began and ended with business.

~*~*~*~

The following day, their conversation included family and friends.

"Joe," Travis said. "I know you stay connected with your siblings. Have you heard of the latest status on Dino?"

"According to family and neighbors back home, he's a changed man."

"Awe, splendid news."

"Yeah, Dino once converted many young mafia wannabes into followers of Christ." Joe paused for seconds and added. "Before he vanished."

"What?" Travis asked as his brows arched. "I'm assuming he moved out of town to escape old mafia connections and took his calling with him?"

"God knows what happened to him."

"I hope he's safe."

Joe shook his head and said, "I hope you're right. Rumors say something dreadful might've happened to him."

"What do you mean?"

"They saw him with strange characters before he vanished."

"I break out in a sweat when I have thoughts of another brush with death, as I experienced in Genoa, Italy," Travis said.

"The mafia's wicked," Joe said. "I'm amazed we're still alive.

My life hung in the balance because these men knew I was your friend. But we must not act so carefree. We're not from Genoa, nearby Dino's territory."

"With Pearl gone and the fall of Dino's empire, he's no problem."

Even though Travis hit a gold mine in the restaurant business, a brighter future awaited. But his memories of Pearl still lingered.

On a late afternoon, after the last customer left, Travis and Joe sat down to enjoy coffee and watch the picturesque view of the Mediterranean Sea.

After Pearl's death, Travis said. "I've lived with agony and confusion. Not the kind everyone might see. My soul weeps. No matter what happens, comfort doesn't show. I've applied my entire energy to the restaurant and placed my soul in His hands."

"An affliction well hidden," Joe said. "I'm surprised you kept your struggles to yourself."

"I knew Jesus stayed close to me. God put learning in my suffering," Travis said. "Pearl went through suffering she couldn't control or overcome. I'm grateful my circle of friends remained close, and you tolerated my disposition."

"Your heart is pure, Travis. You treat your employees with respect and kindness. I have no doubts about you, my friend," Joe said.

Waves of emotion wash over me as though they might drown me. If Joe could view my heart, he'd see how slowly my healing has come. And how I journey through rough waters filled with unknowns.

Travis envisions his life without Pearl, his beloved, in a mysterious way.

Travis prayed under his breath. 'Lord, when I mistakenly held you accountable for my dearest friend's demise, I lost my inner peace. Please, forgive me, Lord. I yearn for your guidance to lead others to your redeeming grace.'

Travis remained a man of prominence, but the sparkle in his blue eyes was gone, although his demeanor remained modest.

Travis's memories often returned to Genoa, and he stayed humble and single. Travis had abundant women after him and had overcome much of his grief. But he still remembered the unforgettable woman he had left behind, a testament to his resilience and strength.

"A hunted soul touched my heart, which affected my life. Pearl's memory still lingers, haunting the places I seldom visit."

Joe glanced at Travis with compassion. "I'm sorry, bro."

Travis matured over the last few months and expected more change.

~*~*~*~

Travis and Joe often enjoyed eating breakfast in their restaurant on Sunday mornings and spent hours conversing.

"Time goes by fast," Travis said. "Several months ago, I learned the details of Pearl's death."

"Time waits for no one. It's time for you to start your quest for a nice Christian woman to fill your void," Joe said. "There're countless women in search of a husband."

Travis smiled." God wired each of us with a void that God can single-handedly fill. Matrimony's not on my agenda. Pearl's love and death still weigh heavy in my heart.

'When I first set foot in Genoa, I had a vision of encountering someone extraordinary, and there she was. The most stunning woman I had ever laid my eyes upon.'

"Pearl reminded me of a free spirit, but she missed her criteria."

"I warned you to look for a mate elsewhere because Pearl belonged to Dino Carino, a mafia boss."

"Yes, I remember."

"In Dino's case, whoever dared to cross him would suffer retaliation," Joe said.

"Dino persuaded Pearl to go with him. He deceived Pearl into believing he helped every girl he took home. But he'd tell them they belonged to him after they stepped inside his place, and they have no place to return to."

"Dino's a master deceiver," Joe said.

Travis removed his cap and scratched his head. "Well, now you know why I wanted Pearl free from Dino."

"Don't judge in such a negative way," Joe said. "I'm not heartless. I wanted to help these young women, but the crisis with Pearl and Dino remained volatile, straining our friendship."

CHAPTER 9~THE EXQUISITE LADY

La Spezia, Italy, 1996

Travis lived to expand his well-known restaurant. Every day, he spent time in the bright kitchen, filled with delicious aromas. Staying busy allowed him to forget his sorrow and loneliness, at least for a while.

Joe kept busy with his pots and pans. Exhaustion claimed them.

Joe moved his yacht to La Spezia, where they both made their temporary home.

On a Monday morning, Travis wrestled with thoughts about Pearl.

"Who can withstand the assault of sustained thinking? If I want to survive, I must get out of this confined place and breathe fresh air," he whispered.

This morning, Travis went to help at the restaurant and found the parking lot full.

I'm glad I came. I'll thank my customers and friends and meet new patrons. The chef might need my help in the kitchen.

Travis worked his way back toward the kitchen, greeting every customer. He sat on a stool to converse with customers, answer questions, and ask questions to get acquainted. Near the back of the restaurant, a young woman sat alone, with long silky black hair, at a small round table-her back to him. Unable to resist, he took a second look.

A sudden sorrow and regret filled his heart. What a coincidence. This woman brings back memories of Pearl, he thought.

Travis gave a deep sigh.

This young woman resembled Pearl. His knees became weak, and a chill swept through him.

The woman turned around, and Travis stopped dead in his tracks, incoherent and speechless.

"How's this possible?"

"Pearl," he whispered.

Pearl fixed her eyes on him and flashed the smile that melted his heart long ago.

"But you drowned," he said.

"Hello," she said, extending her hand. "I'm the Queen of Sheba." Her voice was pleasant. "I suppose you're Alexander the Great?"

Travis held on to the table to balance himself. His head reeled, and his words didn't make sense. The terrifying waves of emotion had returned. They were tumbling him back into the depths of the icy waters.

"Have you come to torment me?" He asked, sat on a chair beside her, and reached to touch her hair. Logic tells you he's lost his mind.

Travis continued, "I grieved for months, believing you'd drown. My intense emotions gave me a reason to kill. I came short of going crazy, which caused me to shun my friend."

"I can't make out what you're saying. Too loud in here," Pearl said.

"You played a terrifying joke on me," he said.

"No joke when you escape from Dino," she said.

Travis paused. "I never saw it coming. What have I done to deserve this?"

"Sorry," Pearl replied. "Give me ten minutes. I can explain."

He stared at Pearl and concluded he had no reason to stay angry.

She'd escaped from her predator, and she was alive.

He realized she needed to move fast and get to a safe place.

Travis reached for her hand and gazed into her eyes.

A moment later, he said. "It's hard to believe you're here. I refuse to step away from this unbelievable delight."

Pearl leaned side long to stroke his cheek.

After realizing what had happened, he took her hand and said, "Let's get out of here."

Before they left the restaurant parking lot, he threw his arms around Pearl and kissed her.

When they relaxed their embrace, Pearl said, "Oh, Travis, I've missed you. Sorry, I didn't inform you, but the transition happened without warning. I've stayed put in my apartment, afraid to jeopardize my life."

Travis drove off, he said. "Tell me the magnificent miracle you experienced."

Pearl gazed out the window, hoping to avoid criticism, and said.

"Okay, but first, I need you to promise me you'll forgive me for what I've done."

"I can't imagine why you'd need my forgiveness," said Travis, "but I promise."

"I faked my death to escape from Dino's place." She glanced at Travis and paused for his reaction.

"What?" he said and laughed aloud. "Tell me your amazing plan to execute your escape," he continued to laugh.

"Dino's aggressiveness terrified me. One day, Dino came after me with a knife. He said it was time to end my life. Frankie forced him to drop the knife."

"I'm happy with your wise decision, but there's no need to apologize. I'm the one who ought to ask for forgiveness. I'm sorry, I didn't protect you and made your captivity worse by challenging Dino."

"You helped me more than you imagined. Do you

remember our talk in the park after spending Saturday together in Genoa? I took those words to heart and transformation took place when I applied God's Word to my life."

"I remember. Tell me how your life has changed."

"Our conversation gave me faith to trust God with my everyday decisions. I know God cares for and values us.

The Lord allows events to happen for a reason. I've noticed a substantial change in you," Travis said with a smile. "I can tell you've matured in the Lord."

"A step at a time." A sigh slipped from her lips. "Yes, God's exceptional."

Travis nodded.

"Travis, remember Frankie?"

"Yes." How can I forget the goon?

"I detested Dino and lived a miserable life. I've grieved every day over it. After you disappeared, I assumed you'd returned home to New York. To this day, I regret that I withheld your cooperation on your rescue mission.

"A weekend came, and Dino left town. Frankie told me he intended to quit the organization once Dino returned. Frankie noticed I'd lost my appetite and was losing weight fast. He asked me if I'd thought of trying to escape again. I shared the possibilities with him and discovered his willingness to help me. He treated me like his sister, and said he lost her to an accident, and I resembled her."

Frankie said he knew the times I was out when I should've been in my room. 'I knew you needed a break," he said. He named a woman Dino went to visit. Dino scheduled his return in three weeks. Frankie offered to help me carry out a getaway plan."

Travis nodded. "What changed in your circumstances that you risked escaping with Frankie's help?"

First, Dino wanted to kill you. And second, Frankie, one of Dino's most trusted men, suggested an escape.

Frankie knew the amount of time he had before Dino returned. Dino contacted him daily.

Frankie gave me the name of the man who was taking his place as my bodyguard when he left. He said he needed more trust in this guy. I took a step of faith and trusted him. The weather forecast reported that a storm would arrive in Genoa any day. He took a trusted friend of his, took Dino's boat miles into the sea, and returned without the vessel. Come daylight, the coastguard found the craft capsized.

"Dino and the Italian authorities thought the waves swept over the boat and ejected me. Frankie made it appear as if it were an accident to keep Dino from searching for me. Freedom came when I least expected it, and I seized the opportunity.

"What a witty idea," Travis said. "You convinced everyone, including me, that you had drowned, and your body was lost at sea."

"Well, I'm still alive." Her heart was beating faster, and her tone of voice grew grim. Even though I thought I'd lost you forever, in my desperation, I moved to Rapallo and prayed you'd find me.

Loneliness filled my heart. A gloom stayed with me and worsened as the months passed.
I've lived in Rapallo for thirteen months with no problems from Dino."

I thought of you every day. And because I came to help in the kitchen, I found you," Travis sighed. I see you have survived, but my question is, how?"

Frankie stuffed cash in an envelope to last a while. He found the apartment and paid for six months' rent. At first, I wandered around and familiarized myself with the surroundings.

"When I ran out of money, I went to eat at the railway station. A religious group feeds those who are homeless. This capillary's presence in winter becomes more necessary for helping helpless people. For specific individuals, the crisis begins at home. They run away and try for independence.

Each stranger has a story. When a soul has lost their home, they seek help. Sometimes, the homeless seek temporary help, but homelessness makes getting a job impossible.

"The wish for an everyday life continues. I know what to expect when you reach the end of the road. That path to recovery starts with a hot meal and a safe place to sleep, which helps to recoup. I slept inside the railway station, where various individuals take shelter for the night.

"This group gives each person a cover and other necessities as needed. People battle to live a dignified life. We enjoy each other for a while, and without warning, they're gone."

"In needy times, any shelter's better than sleeping on the street," Travis said.

"Yes," she said, trembling with hope and uncertainty. "I joined the group. They offered me meals and a safe place to sleep for minor jobs. My plans to get a different apartment encouraged me to work hard. After two weeks, they hired me to work in the office. The expectations of finding you someday kept me going."

"Tell me what happened to you."

"When you refused to meet with me, I returned home to America. To return home is a welcome thought for certain people, but Italy lies half across the world for me. My face showed strength to people, but in secret, it exposed a heart tearing itself to pieces for the lack of you.

"Destiny called me back to Genoa to finish school. A wish to open a restaurant still burned in my soul. And I missed you. After finishing school and polishing my skills, I visited Dino to plead for your release. The news Dino gave me came as a dagger to my heart.

"Conversations can, without warning, go wrong, and we find we're navigating treacherous minefields. I learned that Joe withheld your accident from me. And to get information from Dino crushed me. How can a person move on when they've lost the most precious treasure of their life?

"The news hardened my heart toward Joe. I avoided my friend for a long time. A month went by two months. My heart cautioned me not to trust him. Three months went by before I forced myself to call Joe. He's my partner in the restaurant business, and I've forgiven him."

"I was worried Dino may have killed you," Pearl said.

"How did you find me?"

"This morning, my boss assigned me to deliver supplies to La Spezia, a block from your place. I noticed the restaurant advertisement, Under New Management. Your name appeared on the Billboard, and I knew I had found you," she said.

"This restaurant came as a surprise. I'm powerless when a good buy comes my way," Travis said. "So, I seized the opportunity to buy this bistro."

A smile crossed both their lips.

"Tell me, who's the lucky man you hang out with these days?"

"The man of my life is you."

"An irresistible woman doesn't stay idle for long."

"Life's not glamorous. I've missed you. Living alone has been a constant battle with loneliness. Do you know how much of me yearns for your presence?" Pearl's voice quivered, and her head dropped. "People need people," she said, her words echoing with a deep sense of longing.

Travis glanced at her. Silence filled the air.

"And what are you trying to say?" he asked.

"The thought of loving another never even flickered

in my mind. I stayed steadfast, but one day, I made the decision to go on a date," she whispered, her voice barely audible.

"Loneliness consumed me. I yearned, oh, how I yearned, for someone to share my thoughts with," she sobbed, her words filled with a deep, unquenchable longing.

A moment of tense silence lapsed, and Travis drove slowly, his mind racing with questions. He desperately needed to understand what she meant and decipher the true nature of her feelings. A persistent nagging in his mind demanded answers. The thought that her dating might be out of duty or pity, leading to potential heartbreak, weighed heavily on him, threatening to consume him.

"You work fast," Travis said.

"I responded to an invitation to dinner."

"I'm trying my best not to read between the lines," he said, his voice tinged with a hint of desperation. "And I refuse to challenge a firm commitment made." His fear of potential heartbreak was intense, his voice trembling with emotion.

Lord, I beg you to help me process the details of why Pearl's back in my life. If her heart belongs to another, it'll bring unbearable anguish. Travis fought his emotions, and his prayer was a silent plea for mercy.

The notion that Pearl, the woman who once held my heart, will remove herself from my life is profound. It promises life, sickness, and health, forsaking others. Seeing her wearing a ring that will bind them together may destroy me. The words stabbed back at him. No, it's inconceivable, he thought, his heart aching with the fear of losing her again.

The taut muscles of Travis's face, usually calm and composed, now quivered with a profound sense of distress. His piercing blue eyes, usually warm, were now clouded with a deep, unsettling uncertainty. He battled with his judgment, his brow furrowed in a struggle of deep thought, his emotions threatening to overwhelm him.

Pearl, her voice choked with tears, sniffled, and wiped her eyes with the back of her hand. She fought to compose herself, to conceal the pain that was threatening to engulf her, but her vulnerability was substantial.

"There's one issue I honor. If you're committed to someone, it's not right for me to interfere in the relationship."

Pearl looked at him and said, "Travis, not a soul has caught my interest. You stole my heart."

They sat in silence.

In turmoil, Travis pulled the car over to the side of the road and hit the curb with a jolt. He turned to face Pearl, his eyes filled with love and fear, and stared into her eyes, searching for answers in their depths.

Pearl gave him a sidelong glance. "Has our relationship ended?" Pearl asked.

"You tell me."

"Ever find a needle in a haystack?"

"Haven't tried," Travis said.

"I engaged in a hopeless search when you vanished on me." She wiped the tears, leaving her face smudged.

His heart aching with the memories of their past, Travis leaned over and kissed Pearl. It was a kiss that held their shared history—a bittersweet mixture of longing and uncertainty.

"I cherish you," he whispered, his voice trembling with fear and love. "You're not just anyone to me. I'll never stop loving you. It's a relief to know you're alive, and I'll fight to survive without you. But the thought of you being alive and, in another man's, arms would shatter me. Yet, I fear our reunion came too late. I've lost you to another."

Travis's disappointment continued, and Pearl's despair brushed over her. She pressed her hands together to still the faint trembling.

"I love you. It's frightening to imagine I may lose you again after what we've meant to each other and what we've experienced together." Pearl looked anxious.

"Why can't we start anew? Our relationship faced doom in Genoa, but the circumstances differ in Rapallo."

"Please, Travis, find it in your heart to forgive me. I've been faithful to you," she pleaded, her voice filled with uncertainty, vulnerability, and hope.

"Have you committed to him?"

"I had a dinner date, not a relationship."

"What do you plan to tell your boyfriend? Or must I hang my heart out to dry?" A muscle in his lean jaw twitched with impatience. "I refuse to spend my days guessing if you'll keep him and drop me."

Pearl stared into the eyes of the man she adored and hoped to soften his stern look. She needed a sign to tell her he trusted her.

Travis found himself in a new relationship, a position he was eager to understand and navigate.

"Before I jump in with both feet, clarify your commitment to your boyfriend."

"I can't picture myself without you. I don't know how to handle this snag, but it's not a big problem."

Travis, his heart heavy with their past, leaned over and lifted her face to his, his touch was gentle yet firm. His lips, once so familiar, rested on hers, a fleeting taste of the love they once shared. Pearl's arms, a source of comfort in their earlier life, crept around his neck, her touch warm and familiar. This kiss, a testament to their enduring love, swept her off her feet in ecstatic delight, the world around them fading into insignificance.

At last, he raised his head; his heart throbbed, the sound echoing in his ears, a reminder of the love they had lost and were now trying to regain.

"Yes, I adore you. I'd give my life for you," he said, his voice tinged with the pain of their past. The challenges they had faced, the misunderstandings and the heartbreak, were not forgotten.

"Never loved another," she said in a soft voice. "When I saw you in the department store, I knew we belonged together."

"If I take you back on trust, can you take me back on faith?" Travis asked, a hint of a smile playing on his lips.

"I love you more than life itself," she said. Pearl drew a deep breath.

"Life's amazing. Minutes ago, life ended for me. But grace has allowed me a fresh start with you."

Travis and Pearl, their hearts filled with renewed hope and a sense of reconciliation, celebrated their new chance to embark on a fresh, revitalized relationship. They were hopeful for the future, but also aware of the challenges that lay ahead.

Travis and Pearl rejoiced in their new chance to enter a renewed relationship.

"The time to meet in dark and secluded places is gone. The fear of Dino learning of our relationship is gone," she said.

Rapallo, a place too close to Genoa for comfort. Travis leaned in, his voice low and serious, "Have you ever considered the potential danger if we were to run into Dino? We must be prepared for the worst."

Pearl said, "If we worry something will happen, it's liable to happen. But I don't expect to see him again."

"Pearl, be realistic. You must face the facts."

"Don't be pessimistic," Pearl said.

Travis ran his fingers through his thick hair. His eyes penetrated hers for a moment. "I'm sorry," he said.

The conversation had turned uncomfortable and intense. Travis hesitated for a minute, his face a mask of conflicting emotions. "It's unfair and rude. I didn't consider your perspective on this matter. Please forgive me," he said, his voice filled with regret and a hint of hope.

"For a moment, I thought you had information on Dino." Pearl faked a smile but refused to make eye contact.

We must be careful where we go, for Pearl's sake.

"We better get back before nighttime arrives," Travis said.

Pearl dominated the conversation on their way back. A warm color appeared on her cheeks. There was a sparkle in her eyes, and her teasing voice relaxed Travis.

Travis ditched the thought of learning more about her courtship with a boyfriend. And Dino's name is, well, not worth mentioning.

"Every ending has a fresh start," Travis said, his voice filled with a mix of hope and uncertainty. He was referring to their decision to give their relationship another chance, a decision that could lead to a new beginning or a painful end.

This conversation gave Travis the confidence to accept and resume the relationship they started in Genoa.

Travis continued his role as Mr. Entrepreneur in La Spezia, a role that had brought him success and financial stability. Meanwhile, Pearl remained faithful to her commitment to the religious group in Rapallo. She'd rented an apartment, owned a car and a phone, and enjoyed her job and freedom. She'd survived and was on the way to a full recovery.

~*~*~*~

September temperatures remained unpredictable in La Spezia. The heat rose to an elevated level, and on Friday night, Travis visited Pearl in her small apartment.

When Pearl led him in, and after a quick kiss, Travis said, "You look gorgeous this evening. Have a specific place you care to go to tonight?"

"No," she said. "Smell something delicious?" Pearl asked with a wide smile.

The aroma of a spicy, delicious American apple pie from the oven filled the apartment, a scent that brought back memories of their shared past. It was a dish that Pearl had always cooked for Travis, a symbol of their love and the comfort they found in each other's presence.

"Yes, apple pie," he said.

"I cooked dinner, too. I plan a serious conversation with you tonight," she said, her voice filled with a mix of nervousness and determination. She had important things to share, things that could potentially change the course of their relationship.

"Sounds critical. We ought to talk first."

"No," she said, "we'll eat first. I'm hungry."

Travis and Pearl sat on the sofa after dinner to enjoy a slice of apple pie. Pearl intended to update Travis on her past actions.

The aroma of a spicy, delicious American apple pie from the oven filled the apartment, a scent that brought back memories of their shared past. Pearl had always cooked it for Travis, a symbol of their love and comfort in each other's presence.

"Yes, apple pie," he said.

"I cooked dinner, too. I plan a serious conversation with you tonight," Pearl said, her voice filled with anxiety and determination. She had important things to share, things that could potentially change the course of their relationship.

"Sounds critical. We ought to talk first."

"No," she said, "we'll eat first. I'm hungry."

Travis and Pearl sat on the sofa after dinner to enjoy a slice of apple pie. Pearl intended to update Travis on her past actions.

She smiled and said, "My heart reminds me. I'm a blessed woman to have you back in my life. I've avoided problems by making quality decisions and choices." God instructed me to honor this relationship with honesty. Life without trouble is impossible, and Jesus told us trials would come.

Travis agreed.

Pearl paused, held her hands together, and tried to stop them from trembling. "It's an awkward moment, but I want to reveal my past and the hostility between Dad and myself."

Travis placed his arm around Pearl's shoulders. "You're not required to reveal your past to anyone. But I'll gladly learn more about your father's social life."

Pearl pulled away and said, "I want you to know the real Pearl Moreno. A stranger may someday try to fill your mind with lies."

"Okay, honey, tell your story. You have my full attention."

Pearl inhaled a deep breath and looked away. "When I first met you, I promised I'd tell you my entire past. But today, the topic's my father."

Pearl paused, gave Travis a nervous look, and stroked her hair behind her ear, a bad habit she did when she was nervous or scared.

"First, I'll tell you the reason I ran away from home."

Travis nodded.

Dad heard a rumor that involved a neighboring boy. He thrashed me, and I ran—my hopes of gaining freedom ended when I stepped into Dino's estate. In the past, I talked to you about my captivity. I missed Dad after running away.

I read books and learned what I had missed in school. One day, I became restless and persuaded Frankie to drop me off at Dad's for the day. I needed closure with Dad. I wanted to start a new relationship with forgiveness and love.

"Frankie said he'd return the following morning and warned me. Be suspicious of everyone at Dino's place and avoid telling them whom you went to visit. Dino will take you back, regardless, and kill your father.

"I found the key I left and let myself into my dad's

house. The weather and the eeriness of the place made me frigid. I stoked the wood stove and warmed the house.

"Dad kept chopped wood in the portal. I managed when I lived there. I knew I'd survive the harshness of winter at Dad's. Nothing had changed."

Pearl wiped the palms of her hands on her skirt.

"When I learned Dad had not come home, I found myself in my old bedroom. My aged duvet, which Mom sewed for me, was folded at the foot of the bed. The bed squeaked when I sat on it, and I became aware of the noise for the first time.

"I glanced around the room. The paint had peeled off the walls. The windows needed new coverings; the rest still looked the same. I crawled into bed and fell asleep with the fireplace flame to light the room."

"Morning arrived, and I found myself alone. The expectations of seeing Dad again and hearing his welcome-back greeting failed and made me fretful.

A severe snowstorm hit the town while I slept. "I stepped into the kitchen and noticed snow-covered windows. I grabbed my dad's jacket from the closet and went to the portal to gather more wood. I saw Dad's car parked under the tree. The car door on the driver's side was open.

"The entire scenario looked eerie. Dad died in his most prized possession, his new car. Because Dad always parked his pride and joy under the carport. He sat, hunched over the steering wheel. I froze. I made my way to the parked car.

"His body sat there the entire night, motionless in the driver's seat, while I waited for him inside the house. Dad experienced a heart attack, according to the autopsy report."

"Oh, darling, I'm sorry you had to face these ordeals alone," Travis said and wrapped his arms around her.

Pearl sobbed. "I wanted to visit him. I should've made my way there while he still lived."

"Darling, you mustn't take the blame for your father's death."

"I'm sure I contributed. And I missed the opportunity to tell him I'd forgiven him and needed his forgiveness." Pearl continued to weep.

"During our lifetime, we often have regrets. Each tear causes us to wonder what might've happened if we had taken a different path.

"Frankie returned to take me back before Dino heard the news. I returned later to clean Dad's house and give away his belongings. Under a pile of bills, I found letters he'd written. Dad completed one. Here's what he wrote."

Pearl pulled out a letter she carried in her bosom. Her hands trembled as she read the words she longed to hear from her dad.

To Perlita, my beloved daughter.

I broke you and ruined your childhood. I regretfully hindered your ability to learn and develop relationships with others. And I've trampled your hope for any young man to come into your life.

The measures I took robbed your mother of the opportunity to play with and enjoy her daughter. I denied you both a playful time in your life and hers because I lacked stability.

Time took a toll on her, and it caused my dear, beloved wife to leave me. My Belle Rose left you behind out of desperation to escape. I tried to give you diligent care after your mother left me. Fear entered my life and stayed my constant companion for years.

The fear lay dormant after you returned from staying with your aunt Rose. I thought I had my affairs under control. But the fear intensified as you grew older. I feared you might leave, too. When you left, the anxiety was unbearable. I had depression, and temptation called me to take my life.

I'm acquainted with the evil person who took your mother from us, and I feared he'd take you away, too. I apologize for neglecting to warn you about the cruelest person on earth. My intuition tells me you might've fallen for his deception, too.

In time, my circumstances changed, and I'm a faithful church attendee, but time doesn't heal every wound. Scars still show their intent. I'm still a lonely man, struggling with what I've done to you. I don't know where you've made your home these days. Otherwise, I'd come looking for you with a humble heart. I love and miss you.

There's one concern I need to discuss, and it's forgiveness. I didn't protect you from me. My child, forgive me for my actions that have hurt you. I have always loved you. I'm a man who needs forgiveness. My angel disappeared and left a hole in my heart, and this empty house grieves for you.

Your lonesome father.

Travis heard Pearl whisper, "Dad, I forgive you." One look into her eyes showed her hidden pain. With this forgiveness, years of painful sorrow melted away.

Travis kissed her and held her tight.

"Dad never spoken a kind word since my mother left," Pearl said. "In this letter, he spoke the language of the heart, the key which opened the gate to love and forgiveness.

"Aunt Rose informed me Dad went to church every Sunday and prayed for my return."

Travis's hand trembled as he reached out, his heart aching for Pearl's pain. He gently brushed her hair from her tear-stained face, his touch a balm for her wounded soul.

Pearl stopped. She'd finished her story and gave

Travis a shy smile.

"I admire your courage to admit your struggles, Travis. Jesus still works on our behalf.
He'll bring healing," Travis said, feeling the warmth of Pearl's understanding and support as she embraced him tightly.

"We'll move forward a step at a time."

"Wonder if the person who lied to Dad knew he had destroyed a family in turmoil. The household affair hung by a thin thread without adding more stress."

"I've waited a lifetime for you. Let's enjoy what we have. The past can't destroy our relationship. It's time to bury old memories," Travis said, his voice filled with determination and love. He pulled Pearl closer to him, symbolizing their renewed bond and commitment to each other.

"Darling, our commitment to each other gets stronger each day.

~*~*~*~

Travis and Pearl spent a serene day; their curiosity piqued as they delved deeper into the lives of their household members the following Sunday.

"Travis," Pearl said, "you haven't mentioned your mother. I want to familiarize myself with your family."

"Well, God knows what happened to my mother. I remember her as a gentle, lovable, and quick-witted lady. One day, she went to visit her sister in the suburbs of New York and didn't return. After she left home, she tried to stay connected with me."

"I had turned ten when my mother, Sabrina O'Connor, left the scene. Although my mother is no longer living with us, she often encouraged me by telling me what I wanted to hear. My dad, Malcolm Steele, raised me in a loving environment. He inspired me to impart decent work wherever I went.

She says you are my son—unique, loved, strong,

brave, bright, and intelligent.

Pearl looked over at Travis to offer a word of comfort, but he kept his focus on a sparrow.

"My father lived what men call a good moral life. His deportment is agreeable, and strangers reject his sobriety, yet it affects him little—a man of integrity with ambitious standards. I never entertained the thought of backing off from these morals. A man who held his own."

"I missed Mom. I never asked for her for fear of changing Dad's demeanor. But my instincts tell me he missed her, too."

"Have you searched for her?"

"With great regret, I don't know where to start."

"Could it be she doesn't either? And have you thought she may have passed?"

"It's possible. My mother moves often, and I don't know where to find her."

Travis had neglected to engage in the thoughts of his immediate family until Pearl mentioned it.

Travis stared into the distance and said, "Dad worked hard to instill positive values and give me a secure life while nurturing me in God's word. I'm grateful for his dedication.

"I learned that the Christian walk is a struggle. And different occurrences compete for our time.

I came to Italy, a place known for its culinary excellence, to equip myself with the skills and knowledge needed to open a restaurant. This decision was not made lightly, but after years of helping in the restaurant business with my dad, I felt a calling to do something more.

Pearl, my confidante, kissed me and said, "You're a skilled chef, Travis. I believe in you and your ability to make the right decisions for your future."

"Well, I've reached a peak in the restaurant business and kept my promise to my father. The successes exceed more than I dreamed possible. It's time to move in a more positive direction."

"I've sensed your interest in serving the public shifting for weeks," she said, her voice filled with understanding. "It's not a terrible thing, Travis, just a change. I'm here to support you, no matter your journey's direction."

"I know it's time to sell my business. I lack the precious time and energy to run a restaurant. But I need someone to help me with marketing and preparing the paperwork. If you're interested in helping, I'll turn the business part over to you when I decide to take the plunge."

"Share your plans with me. What will you do after selling the restaurant?"

"The Holy Spirit nudges me each day to start a ministry."

We'll talk more when I have a more serious plan.

Travis wanted to tell Pearl about his plans to build a building and hold Sunday services, but he was worried about her reaction and stayed quiet.

"Honey," he said, "go with me to Rome for a week?"

"I'll call and make reservations. I need time alone with you, away from the hustle and bustle."

Pearl smiled. "A promise of fun and excitement. I'll take pictures."

Travis smiled and hugged her. "That's my girl."

CHAPTER 10~DEATH TRAP

La Spezia

When Travis and Pearl returned from their vacation, he returned to his obligation, the restaurant, and she returned to the rewarding job she loved and appreciated.

Spending time together has become difficult for Travis and Pearl. Their workload denies them the pleasure of being together, often leaving them feeling specific emotions. When the occasion allows them to meet, they grieve to see the day end. But their commitment to each other grew more assertive, even during career challenges.

They nurtured a tender and profound love for each other, a love that consumed their secret world, leaving the rest of the universe unnoticed. It was a rare love that people spend their lives in search of.

A week later, in the late afternoon, Travis visited Pearl. He carried a basket full of customer complaints, each a unique challenge he had to face, but he also had excellent ideas for starting a ministry.

"I've chosen this time to tell you what I'm planning."

"Have you kept another secret from me?" She asked, her voice tinged with a specific emotion.

"I'm struggling with a huge decision. Owning a restaurant generates excitement and brings in wealth. But my interests lie in another venture."

"Tell me the entire story this time," Pearl said.

"I'm exhausted in the restaurant business."

"You're doing great in the family business. You're

zealous in your work and selfless with your customers. People enjoy coming around to visit with you."

"As a business owner, I have excellent benefits. But tough decisions fall on my shoulders."

"I take pleasure in hearing how people enjoy eating in my restaurant.

"As a local businessperson, I met motivating people.

Your friends are interested, even if your restaurant is outside your hometown. A restaurant is a neighborhood-pleasing gathering spot.

"I've met people that I call friends and individuals that I treasure as members of my household."

"You have a sympathetic approach and an excellent demeanor as a business owner.

"To manage a restaurant reminds me of nurturing a child," Travis said. "Who takes more interest and pride than you in such matters? But worry and stress come with owning a business. There are drawbacks to consider. Including long days and nights and kissing your weekends goodbye. The weekend is a busy time in a restaurant."

"Why haven't you told me how this problem affected you?"

Travis reached for Pearl's hand, and a frown formed on his forehead.

"My decision came with powerful emotions."

"When you're home, plan on being on the phone with employees all day. I turned off my phone in Rome and returned to a plate full of complaints."

"I'm sorry to hear you've had so much trouble, but you must stay in touch with your employees. It's part of a business."

"I entered this business enterprise with wide-open eyes and occupied myself with restaurant equipment and unreliable employees. You're back in my life, and the restaurant doesn't allow me to spend time with you."

~*~*~*~

Pearl cuddled closer and approved of Travis's plans.

"I want to honor the one I share my plans with. Would you like to take a ride to Genoa with me?"

"Genoa!" Pearl said.

"Don't worry. Dino's moved on. He doesn't live in Genoa anymore," Travis reassured, his voice filled with relief.

"Okay, if you promise."

Travis took her hand. "Come on, let's go."

Travis drove to Genoa, parked far from where he was taking Pearl, and had to walk two blocks.

Pearl smiled when she realized the jewelry store was the destination.

Travis had made prior arrangements to have the owner open after hours.

"Yes," Travis said. "This is my gorgeous lady."

The jeweler smiled and hurried behind the jewelry case, pulling out a stunning, luminous, three-carat, pear-shaped engagement ring. A small diamond on each side matched and complimented the large stone.

Travis forced his eyes on Pearl, eager for her reaction.

Pearl's mouth dropped in surprise. "It's gorgeous," she said, her voice filled with awe.

"Allow me to place it on your finger," Travis said, his voice quivering with anticipation, his hands trembling. "Before I place this diamond on your finger, make sure you want this one. The jeweler will allow you to change your mind for another you prefer."

"You picked an excellent one."

Travis kneeled on one knee in front of her. "Pearl, will you marry me?" he asked, his voice shaky.

Pearl's eyes moved from the ring to Travis's eyes. Pearl gazed at him with tear-filled eyes. She threw her arms around him. Travis's lips rounded into a beautiful smile.

"Yes, yes, yes," she said. "I'll marry you."

Tears of overwhelming joy streamed down Pearl's

face. She had the man of her dreams, and he loved her. Life was now a canvas of new joy, free from running, insecurity, or fear.

"Congratulations," the jeweler said. And Pearl walked out with an extra extravagant ring.

"Let's go around the corner to get a bite to eat at the small restaurant where we dined on our first date."

Pearl agreed.

Travis remembered he'd left his billfold in the car as they entered the restaurant. He dashed back while Pearl stood in line. Her eyes focused on the menu on the wall, undecided and awaiting Travis.

Pearl felt someone touch her neck. His breath was hot on her neck. The stranger whispered in her ear. "At last, we meet again," he said.

Pearl recognized the voice, and fear pierced her soul. She tried to move away from the intruder, but he gripped her elbows tight. "Turn me loose!" Pearl demanded.

The smarting sheathed her entire body as she tried to pull her arm away, forcing herself loose from his tight grip. She swung around to see Dino standing next to her.

"It's you?"

Dino stared at her. "Surprised? Yes, it's me. Sorry, I startled you. Oh, Amore, you duped me into believing you drowned? The games you play are so deceitful and hard to accept."

The strength drained out of her limbs. Pearl's fearful eyes showed defeat.

Dino's aware I'm alive and knows I deceived him. The end of my life has arrived, she thought. The preparations, goals, and my life with Travis all fall around me like cards.

"Why can't you leave me alone?" Pearl asked. "You have dominated my life and caused me extreme misery."

Dino smiled and showed his last few rotten teeth. "I'm pleased you've come back among the living."

Pearl thought Dino's gentle tone had an underlying malice. Travis, please hurry back. You're my hope in this danger, a danger that could potentially cost me my life.

Pearl backed away from Dino. His breath and his filthy clothes emitted an awful stench.

"Oh, Amore, it's a miracle you're alive. I'll confess that when they told me you'd drown, I tried suicide. But today, I've found you. Return with me, and we'll start afresh. I don't want any trouble."

"You stay away from me," Pearl warned, glancing toward the entrance.

The soda shop's customers, a mix of regulars and passersby, included women and their children. Anxious mothers, sensing the tension in the air, pushed their young ones out the door to avoid confrontation, getting ready to unfold right before their eyes. Once filled with chatter and laughter, the shop fell into an uneasy silence as everyone's attention turned to Pearl and Dino.

"Oh, Lord, please help us." Pearl prayed in a whisper.

Dino mellowed out and said, his voice dripping with false sweetness, "Leave your hair alone, Amore. I have no intention of harming you. Let's sit and have coffee for old times' sake. I'm confident you've experienced feelings like mine. Our attraction to each other's reality." Pearl, her heart pounding in her chest, tried to steady her trembling hands as she considered her options.

"A psychotic person imagines the unthinkable," Pearl said.

Dino's tone of voice became hostile. "After what we have gone through together, you're still naïve. I've found you and am taking you back to my place. When I claim a woman, she's mine forever.

"I'll call home, and they'll throw you a welcome-back party."

"Your ideas are ludicrous," Pearl said, stepping

backward in disbelief.

Dino reached for her arm. In his struggle with Pearl, he shot a glance toward the entrance. Someone caught his eye, which caused him to dash out of the restaurant's back exit and disappear.

Pearl looked toward the door, and there stood Travis, rubbing his chin, confused because the customers had left. When he read what had happened, he gave chase after Dino.

When Travis returned, Pearl ran to him and said, "Dino's found me. He won't stop until I'm dead."

"Relax, honey—Dino's alone. Every man, including his servant, has left him. And he's a coward when he's alone."

"Dino knows I'm alive. He wants to take me back to his place," she gasped and shrank against him.

"Dino better act wise before he tries to take you back," Travis said. He walked to the window, and looked around, hoping to see Dino. He abandoned his pursuit when darkness drew a veil around the city.

Pearl took his hand and said, "Let's go home, honey."

"I'm taking a restraining order on Dino and calling the local authorities on him."

"Dino's not worth the price you'll pay. And I'm afraid an injunction won't matter much to him. He defies authority every chance he gets. It's another challenge for him."

"I had hoped he'd be a different man when I saw Dino again. Transformation takes more than saying you'll adjust your life. A change must take place," Travis said.

"Yes, the same repulsive deeds of his past have resurfaced.

~*~*~*~

Pearl feared Dino might follow them back to Rapallo, where she lived alone.

"Honey, you'll stay with me tonight," Travis said. "I'm sorry we went to Genoa. Rumors circulated that Dino no longer lived in Genoa."

"Honey, we don't know when and where he'll be present."

"Dino's less dangerous. But he can sure make our lives miserable," he said.

"Travis, he's still a dangerous man. And despite his waspish attitude, he's witty. Someone needs to pluck out his sting and call the police."

Travis noticed a car approaching them fast and passing them at high speed. "Wow, the maniac's putting others in danger by speeding."

He looked like Dino, he thought. The unexpected happened. The stranger pulled off the road and waited for Travis and Pearl to come around the bend.

After seeing a man standing by his car pointing an enormous weapon in their direction, Pearl yelled, "Travis, look out!"

The shots rang out as they came into sight. Travis heard a blast, and the windshield shattered into a million pieces. The shooter shot every window out. Their vehicle went out of control and sent them spinning toward the gorge.

The car hit a boulder before going into the ravine and coming to a stop. The accident caused glass fragments to scatter around them, on the seats, clothes, and floor.

Dazed and confused by the impact, Travis thought he might black out. Moments later, Travis heard the rumbling of a car approaching. The assailant crept through the accident scene at a snail's pace, with headlights turned off and running lights on in low visibility.

This person passed them minutes before, at ninety miles an hour. This same individual shot to kill and waited to survey the damage he'd caused.

"Get out of the car and run. He's coming after us.

Take cover behind the boulder. He'll shoot to kill if he knows we're still alive.

"Babe, we must move fast. Pearl, Pearl," he said, but there was still no answer. In the mishap, Travis lost his phone, which triggered fear. Travis remembered Pearl owning a phone. He searched and found it in her shirt pocket.

Travis pulled Pearl out of the car, ditched it, and hid behind a boulder.

The assailant revved the engine as he drove past the scene.

Travis dialed 911.

"Lorenzo Romano," a voice on the other end said, "Come Posso aiutarla?"

The acting chief of police, Lorenzo Romano, answered the chilling call.

"This call is an emergency!" Travis cried, "A car accident occurred when a sniper shot at us and hit my girlfriend. We're between Genoa and Rapallo, right after the big bend. Please hurry. She's unconscious and bleeding." I'm afraid to move her.

A short while later, the ambulance arrived and found them unconscious. The paramedics loaded them and raced to a local hospital.

Travis spent thirty minutes in the emergency room before someone addressed him. His thoughts and prayers remained with Pearl, and he blamed himself for taking her to Genoa.

At last, a nurse appeared. Travis prayed in silence. "Please, Lord, bring me good news. Pearl has faced adversity her whole life. We live in a sad world of gloom."

Travis watched the nurse prepare to take his vitals. He braced himself and asked what he wanted to know.

"How's Pearl?

"Her condition remains the same," the young nurse said.

Travis gave the nurse his full attention. His heartbeat raced for fear she'd face dire complications.

"She's facing surgery. I don't have any other details," the nurse added.

~*~*~*~

Every chance Travis had; he'd check on Pearl's status.

"After removing a nasty bullet that lodged at the top of her shoulder, your lady friend's stable," the doctor said.

"Is she conscious?" Travis asked.

"We gave her morphine to keep her comfortable. We've ruled out any internal injuries that might've occurred on the impact."

"Pearl will have a quick recovery. And in your case, you'll survive. I'd love to answer every question, but they expect me at the surgery room in five minutes." The doctor said and left.

The nurse came in, smiled, and fussed over him.

"Excuse me," Travis said, his voice above a whisper. "I need to make an urgent plea."

"Yes, how can I help you?"

"Pearl must have protection. The shooter might return and kill her if she's left alone."

"Pearl's under constant watch. But I'll tell the doctor when I see her. Your statement is a strong claim."

"Okay, let's focus on you," she said. "The knot on your head comes from hitting a sharp object. And I'm waiting for the x-rays on your ribs to come back. When the report comes in, I'll let you know."

Please help me lay on my other side. "My back is tender to the touch, but the acute discomfort has subsided."

"It's a positive sign that rules out internal injuries," she said.

"Breathing's difficult. I need a painkiller."

"It's expected if you have broken ribs. We must wait. We'll give you medication when we know what we're treating."

The nurse checked his temperature. "The doctor may give you ibuprofen to take at home."

"I will return," the nurse said. Travis followed her every step with his eyes. He prayed, "Lord, please bless Pearl with a speedy recovery. We need your grace and healing. Please help us."

The powerful force of emotion overpowered him. He couldn't control his feelings. Travis buried his face in his hands and wept. "Lord, have you abundant us?"

The nurse returned and stood beside the bed, watching him. "Travis," she said, "be still. Your injuries will worsen if you don't stop your fussing."

After hours, the doctor returned to speak to him. Travis gave her his full attention.

"Pearl's still in intensive care," the doctor said. "I expect to move her to a room within an hour."

Travis's shoulders dropped, relieved. A great blessing and a burden lifted. "Can I see her?"

"Not until she's in her room."

The nurse saw his disarray, and the rails went up on his bed.

The following morning, the nurse returned to check his vitals.

Travis rubbed the sleep from his eyes.

"I hope you slept well last night," she said with a smile.

"You must've drugged me last night."

"The doctor ordered a sedative to relax you."

"I don't take drugs," he said. "And I manage well with little sleep."

"There's another light sedative tonight to help you ride out the night," she said.

"I don't need drugs to sleep."

The nurse smiled.

"I want to visit Pearl," he said.

"You must stay in bed and not move so much."

Travis insisted on seeing Pearl.

"Ok," the nurse said. "I'll take you."

Travis stared at Pearl, motionless, in the recovery room. The doctor wrapped half of her torso, shoulder, and arm. Tubes stuck out of her body.

"It looks serious," Travis said.

The nurse smiled.

"So many wires," he said.

The doctor walked into the room.

"I plan to remove the wires and tubes this week. I'll give Pearl a complete assessment and watch her closely. Pearl's coming along as expected."

Minutes passed, and the doctor excused herself, and the nurse wheeled him back to his room.

Travis longed to see those blue eyes open. He recalled Pearl saying that our eyes are the windows to our souls.

Travis pleaded with the Lord. "I pray Pearl might have a speedy recovery, and please protect her from Dino. Lord, months have passed since Pearl, and I started a new relationship. We've lived by your rules. Why can't we get past Dino?"

Travis asked every nurse who checked his vital signs if Pearl showed any improvement.

The staff gave him the same report. Healing comes slowly.

Then, the doctor consented for Travis to visit Pearl.

Travis tried to jump off the bed, but the nurse scolded him.

It surprised him when he kissed Pearl, and there was no response. He returned the following morning, and Pearl smiled. She looked like a million dollars to him.

~*~*~*~

On Wednesday morning, they arrived. The doctor explained to Travis what he'd need at home when she released him. "Most broken ribs heal within six to eight weeks. Patients can return to work and leisure activities within six to eight weeks." The doctor said: "You have five broken ribs, which might take longer. You can go home today."

"Aren't you going to tape my ribs?"

"No, we can't set broken ribs in a cast. They can't be immobile, like other bones. It will prolong the healing. Your ribs move every time you take a breath. Over time, the fracture heals, and the pain goes away, but rib fractures, like any fracture, hurt.

"You can take Tylenol to ease discomfort. Over-the-counter painkillers work well. I'll give you a prescription if you don't get relief."

Before his release, the local police met with Travis. "Mr. Steele, I need to know if you recognized the shooter."

"I know Dino Carino opened fire on our car last night," Travis explained of the life Pearl lived under Dino before she escaped. He also included the altercation with Dino minutes before the accident.

"Mr. Steele," the officer said. "We may need to talk to you again."

~*~*~*~

On the day of his release, he called a cab to take him to rent a car and returned to the hospital. He moaned and groaned with pain from the five fractured ribs he'd received. He did not convince the doctor to allow him to take Pearl home.

"I'm sure she'll recover faster at home," he pleaded.

"She might go home in a couple of days," the doctor said.

Pearl nodded and gave Travis an angelic smile.

The Italian authorities questioned Pearl. She reported her captivity under Dino and the brutal treatment she had experienced. And she mentioned the reason he might kill her.

"The owner of the high-powered weapon reported it stolen," Officer Draghi said. "This individual can do grave damage with this dangerous weapon. We must find him. We'll keep you informed."

The authorities continued to investigate and search for the shooter. But Travis and Pearl knew Dino's decadent mind. And they placed awareness at the top of their list.

~*~*~*~

"Honey," Pearl said, her voice trembling with urgency on the drive back to La Spezia, "we must hurry and get married."

"It may shed new light on Dino's thoughts of ownership," Travis said.

They went through a period of recovery. Life was full of joy and contentment, but she feared her shadow.

Travis thought Pearl needed to conquer her fear. This fear, a constant companion, causes intense discomfort, reaching a peak within minutes, including sweating, shaking, and shortness of breath when she's alone, leaving her feeling utterly vulnerable.

"I'm concerned this might impair long-term memories and cause damage to parts of her brain, "Travis thought, his determination to help Pearl clear in his mind. "I must help her overcome fear and interest her in productive activities."

"Honey, you can start preparing for the restaurant sale whenever you feel better," Travis said.

"Thank you!"

Travis pulled her closer to him. "Yes, I won't have to worry that you're home alone while I'm at work. You'll be with me."

He thought Pearl would not find peace until the authorities captured Dino and incarcerated him. Pearl knows Dino wants to kill her. I must make her surroundings safe.

"Darling," Travis said urgently. "I've hired a private detective to investigate Dino's criminal records. Mr. Mares will probe around where others cannot, and we need his help as soon as possible."

"The police can manage this case."

"Mr. Mares enjoys life and works hard. He's in his late thirties and considered a workaholic."

Travis smiled. "His associates know him as Eagle Eye. He has complete control of a case because he doesn't miss a dot and turns subjects inside out. And even a speck gets inspected.

"You'll meet him this afternoon. He's a family-oriented person.

And a straight and honest ex-cop, willing to help us. We need hard evidence to put Dino behind bars. To depend on the local authorities is ridiculous. Eagle Eye will work on our behalf. He's eager to make his name known.

"Eagle Eye can find state and local criminals, retrieve, analyze, examine criminal records, knock on doors, and find witnesses. He can interview witnesses for a civil or criminal lawsuit. He can help manage sensitive cases and perform other duties. If anyone can find solid evidence to keep Dino behind bars, he can."

"Cases with the same status as ours seldom take priority. It may lack credibility," she said.

"The detective will keep us informed. Someone must act against Dino. But we're fortunate to have found this young and energetic detective. I'll have Eagle Eye work on Dino's case while we plan our wedding and sell the restaurant."

~*~*~*~

"When you start your ministry, you can bring others to Christ, Pearl said. And express
Christ's righteousness through your personality."

"The Holy Spirit will guide me. I want to stress God's power in His Son and emphasize that it's not man's devices we must trust. A particular group of people ignore God's word in different areas of their lives. I want God to transform people's lives."

"Admire your zeal," Pearl said, "and I'm excited to know your plan. After we're married, I'll welcome the challenge of helping in your ministry.

"I have an idea. You can allow Joe to manage your restaurant. He's unattached and capable and will take pleasure in the challenge. Joe can run the restaurant and stay on top of the market."

"Great idea," Travis said. "Joe's far from getting married. Joe considers his skills limited to the kitchen, but I know he's a high-class individual. Joe has great patience with the employees. This restaurant has had rapid growth. He has created a pleasant environment and made us wealthy.

"I'm excited. I'll call Joe tomorrow and make the offer."

The following morning, Travis presented Joe with his proposition.

"Glad to help," Joe said. "But I want you to consider me the person most interested in buying your restaurant. If we can negotiate a price, I'd buy this restaurant. It supports itself with locals who have become my friends. I'll succeed here."

They agreed on the terms within minutes, and Travis said, "I'll have Pearl start the paperwork."

Travis turned off the phone and said, "What's next on our agenda?"

"Our next step is the most exciting one," she said, her voice filled with anticipation. "Our
vows. The moment we've been waiting for is the beginning of our new life together."

CHAPTER 11~WEDDING BELLS

La Spezia.

The weather was warmer than usual on this overcast day, and Pearl had plans.

"Honey," Travis said. "Make sure you buy the prettiest gown for your wedding."

Her eyes glittered. "Marriage, what an opportunity to honor God, she said."

"It's a reason to marry right away."

Pearl's face looked radiant, a burst of sunshine on a cloudy day.

"We don't need to have an expensive wedding."

Travis glanced at her. "What's the plan?"

"We can celebrate with our dearest friends and beloved family," Pearl said, her voice filled with warmth. She leaned into Travis's embrace, her body fitting perfectly against his.

"The way you nestle into my arms is pure magic," he whispered, his lips brushing against hers. "From the moment you first embraced me, I knew I had found my perfect match. You ignite a fire within me."

Without a doubt, their commitment to each other continued to flourish and thrive. Pearl's heart raced with anticipation. "Today, I embark on the most thrilling shopping spree of my life. I'm out to find the perfect wedding gown."

Pearl turned her face to hide a tear, but Travis noticed.

"What's the matter, honey?" he asked.

Pearl smiled. "I'm fine, but she refused to make eye

contact.

"No, no, no, what's wrong? I must've missed vital information," Travis said.

"To marry you is an answer to my prayers."

"Why so dejected?"

"When most brides go to buy their wedding gown, their mother or best friend joins them on that special day. No mother or special friend can help me pick out my gown."

"Oh, baby, I'm sorry. I'll go with you."

"The groom must avoid seeing the bride in her gown until she walks the aisle to the altar. It's the tradition," she said, smiling apologetically at him.

"I'll wait outside or in the lobby," Travis suggested.

Pearl glanced at Travis. Her eyes were full of tears. "Yes," she said. "I'll accept your offer."

"Here's a blank check," Travis told Pearl. "Marriage happens once in a lifetime. Make sure you don't hold back."

Pearl had prepared to spend the entire morning at the bridal shop. But after she tried on two gowns, Pearl told the sales consultant, "I love simplicity in clothes. I've decided on the silk gown with a pearl front. The longer I'm here, the more perplexed I get and spend more."

"I approve of the Sabrina neckline," the consultant said. "It's not a simple gown. I can assure you the dress is elegant with a high price tag."

Pearl smiled. "I will take the tiara with the tiny pearls and the medium-length veil."

The consultant nodded. "Excellent," she said. The veil goes with this gown."

"I'm undecided whether to wear short gloves or long. Give me your opinion," Pearl said, her voice filled with uncertainty.

"Long gloves are a perfect choice."

~*~*~*~

Pearl's concerns over the day of the event caused

her face to break out. She thought it must be the mental
strain of preparing for marriage.

"What if Dino shows his face during our marriage
ceremony?"

"The men can oversee it," Travis said. "And I'll
keep my eyes open for any disturbance."

"What can you do without placing yourself in
danger?" And do you plan to leave me alone at the altar
while you chase Dino?"

"It's not happening," Travis said with a smile. "But
there're times when catching a fox takes on an air of
vulnerability."

"Travis, you're not funny. With a high-powered
weapon, he might kill our guests and us."

"Dino's such a dangerous and unpredictable man,"
Joe said.

Travis considered the matter dangerous and warned
everyone to keep their eyes open for Dino and to stay alert
and watchful."

After contemplating this idea, Travis said, "We must
not wait for Dino to show his face and cause trouble. We
must take drastic steps to protect everyone involved. The
problem won't go away until we defeat his tactics."

"Tell me how to defeat his tactics?"

"By being smart and taking precautions,"

The power of silence captured the moment. With a
puzzled look on Pearl's face, she said,
"Dino's still corrupt, and he's far away from God's
principles. He's more dangerous. You'll need Police
Officers to stand at the door.

"To kill another person won't faze him but will add
more to his lengthy list of victims.

"Must secure this property," Joe said.

"Dino has instilled fear in our lives for much too
long. To sit, wait, and allow him to make the first move is
madness," Travis said. "An officer at each corner will do

the job."

Travis and Pearl had planned the wedding in a couple of weeks. Everyone involved remained nervous.

~*~*~*~

"I must deliver my aunt's invitation in person," Pearl said, her voice tinged with anticipation and concern. "Will you drive me there? You two must get acquainted." A poignant moment unfolded for Pearl and her Aunt Rose as they reunited after years of separation. The toll of time was clear on her aunt's health, a stark contrast to the vibrant woman Pearl remembered. Yet, despite her frailty, her aunt's eyes sparkled with delight at the prospect of attending the wedding, a bittersweet reminder of the fleeting nature of life.

"Time gets away from us," Rose said. "Time steals our years away. It etches wrinkles on our faces, scribbles crow's feet around our eyes, and paints our hair white. Yes, time waits for no one."

"You look charming," Pearl said, her voice filled with a deep, bittersweet nostalgia that resonated with her aunt's frailty. As she gazed at Aunt Rose, the last living link to her past, a powerful wave of emotions crashed over her. Where has the time gone? Her once sturdy aunt now uses a wheelchair. These thoughts, like a drumbeat in her chest, caused her heart to palpitate.

Apart from minor distractions, the marriage ceremony went as planned. Every detail fell into place. With a touch of nostalgia, Pearl displayed a unique burlap and lace guest book for people to sign. This book, a symbol of their journey together, was a testament to the love and support they had received from their friends and family. Each signature and each message was a cherished memory of their loved ones who had seen their union.

"I'm amazed Dino stayed away on our special day," Pearl said, a hint of concern in her voice. Dino, a figure from their past, had always made his presence felt, even in his absence. His non-appearance on their wedding day was a relief and a cause for curiosity. Dino, a man with a mysterious past and a penchant for causing trouble, had been a constant source of tension in their lives.

"I hope he searches his heart and leaves us alone. He may move to another country."

Pearl opened her mouth to give her opinion. Travis, always the one to calm her, put his finger across her lips. "Shush," he said, his voice filled with love and understanding. He hugged her and planted a kiss on his wife's lips. It was a silent promise, a reassurance that they would face whatever came their way together.

Travis changed the topic, his voice filled with excitement. "Well, my darling wife, are you ready to embark on our grand adventure to our secret island for our honeymoon? I want to honor our commitment by creating a perfect ending to our wedding saga, a memory that will last a lifetime."

And the couple disappeared for ten days on their mystery island.

~*~*~*~

After Travis and Pearl returned from their honeymoon, Travis heard a frantic cry from the backyard. He raced out to see what caused Pearl to scream. There, in the once serene garden, lay a scene of devastation. The flowers, once vibrant and full of life, were now trampled and broken. It was a malicious deed, a clear sign that someone had trespassed with ill intent.

"Someone has trampled on my flowers and destroyed them."

"They're not dead," Travis said. "A couple of plants may need replacing."

He wrapped his arms around her. "I'll plant new ones again."

Travis tried his best to calm her. The incident left him with unanswered questions.

"Dino's the culprit of this malicious deed," she said, her voice trembling with fear and uncertainty. "Dino knows where we live, and he'll harass me the rest of my life."

"Honey, you don't know if Dino caused this. It might've been a dog claiming his territory."

"No. It's not a dog's print, I see. Look here, a shoe print," Pearl said, her voice taking a higher pitch. "We must report this incident."

"Yes, we must," Travis said.

The local police filled out a report of an unknown person trespassing on private property.

Pearl squeezed her eyes shut and prayed that the authorities would find the person who wished to invade her paradise.

Travis called Eagle Eye, a private investigator they had hired to keep an eye on Dino and informed him of the incident. Eagle Eye, a man with a reputation for his keen observation skills and ability to solve mysteries, was their last hope in this escalating situation.

"Dino's spying on us makes the occurrence crucial so that we find another place to live."

"To move every time will please Dino," Eagle Eye said. "But you must take safety measures."

"We've become prisoners in our own home. Dino has a lethal wish for us."

"Dino's out to destroy more than Pearl's plants or her tranquility," Eagle Eye said, his voice filled with concern. "I see a warning sign in this invasion. It's obvious. The problem will escalate from this point. Dino, a man with a dark past and a grudge to settle, was not one to back down easily. The invasion of their home was just the beginning, a sign of things coming.

"We've become prisoners in our own home. Dino has a lethal wish for us."

"Dino's out to destroy more than Pearl's plants or her tranquility," Eagle Eye said. "I see a warning sign in this invasion. It's obvious. The problem will escalate from this point."

"Strange, Dino continues to take chances but must know I'm home. It makes me wonder what's on his mind."

"He's not afraid of you if he has a powerful weapon," Eagle Eye said. "This circumstance has become unsafe for you and Pearl."

"We received a phone call when we first arrived back from our honeymoon, but no one answered on the other end.

"I suppose Dino wanted Pearl to answer the call to harass her."

"Travis, you must be careful. Dino wants you out of the way."

~*~*~*~

The following week, Travis's days turned nerve-wracking. A man of faith, Travis appeared nervous on the first day of the month and had a nippy morning, a stark contrast to his usual calm demeanor.

"We must depend on God's promise and act like His children."

Jesus said, "I'm the light of the world. So, we must make sure we stay focused on His light. The promises of God, a beacon of hope, offer a sure foundation for those who trust Him. Heaven knows we haven't trusted in Him with Dino. We must not take our eyes off God's grace and question His goodness," Travis said, his voice filled with conviction.

"What a fearful thought when we go under the x-ray vision of Jesus Christ," Pearl said. "I ask God for mercy. I pray He'll say, Well done, good and faithful servant. Enter the joy of your Lord.

"I've tasted grace and can't wait to tell the world how God delivered me from death. I wish I'd known Him before I escaped from Dad," Pearl said with a tear. "I'll share this experience with everyone I meet, hoping it'll

thread itself into their lives and give me peace. And they'll
live closer to God."

~*~*~*~

The weeks went by fast, and the ministry blossomed.
At times, they had to divert their attention to safety.

"God is good. He has allowed us to soar high on
wings like eagles." Travis said.

"To trust in the Lord means to find new strength,"
Pearl said.

"That's God's promise. If we are believers, we must
be depended on His word."

Travis, having delivered five sermons, was drawn to
a woman who carried an air of mystery. She was a regular
attendee, always deep in prayer, and Travis, intrigued by her
enigmatic presence, had made her one of his favorite
members.

She sat in the front row every Sunday, her posture
straight and her hands clasped in prayer. After the service,
she would linger, her eyes downcast, lost in thought. But
she never made eye contact with Travis, always seeming to
be in her own world, a world he was eager to understand.

"It's unbelievable," Travis told Pearl, shrugging. "I
make myself available after every service. This woman
avoids me."

"But she's irresistible and meek." Compelled to talk
to her, Travis said, "I'll have to make the first move," his
voice filled with determination and anticipation.

On Sunday, Travis, determined to break the
woman's silence, came to give a sermon. "Thank you for
your faithfulness in your attendance. The congregation's
blessed to have you join us for Sunday worship." The
woman, her eyes filled with surprise and uncertainty, looked
up. "Thank you, it's my pleasure," she said, her voice soft
but steady.

"Thank you, it's my pleasure," the woman said with
a wide smile.

"When I heard your longtime dream to serve the Lord had come true, I had to see it myself."

"Sorry, do we know each other?" Travis asked.

"Many moons have passed since we shared a conversation," the woman replied.

"May I ask your name?"

The woman ignored his question. "I've warred with my spirit to come

and converse with you, but I found myself unworthy every time. I'm glad you reached out."

"Have I intimidated you?" Travis asked with a smile.

The woman returned his smile and said, "My name is Sabrina, Sabrina O'Connor."

Travis stared at the woman and said, "I'm sorry, but I can't place you."

"I expected this might cause you some problems."

"I want to welcome you to God's house."

The woman disregarded his welcome and continued, "I've made many mistakes in my life."

"Everyone makes mistakes," Travis said. "But God wants to forgive the worst blunders we've carried out. God's Grace is unlimited, although we must come to Him for mercy."

Her manner appeared to suggest that she wanted to confess her deeds and ask God for forgiveness. Travis prepared to tell her how God pardons and gives everyone a new life.

He guessed the truth and understood the circumstances. This woman wanted to admit her guilt and ask Travis for forgiveness.

"The past few weeks, I've learned to appreciate you more," she said.

The statement surprised him. "Your presence has blessed the church members," Travis said.

"Time or disaster will not destroy God's Grace. You

can't buy Grace for any price. God gives this gift to everyone who belongs to Him. God gives Grace and loving favor to those he has rescued. Without Grace, no person sees salvation."

This woman didn't hear a word, he said. She wanted to tell her story.

"I've changed my last name back to O'Connor from Steele. What does Sabrina Steele mean to you?"

For seconds, Travis remained silent. He reached out and placed his hands on Sabrina's shoulders. Travis's voice quivered. "You're my mother?"

"Yes," she said, tears filling her eyes. "The first day I arrived here, I wanted to take you in my arms and hold you tight like I did when you needed love as a child. The fear that my son may not acknowledge me, as his mother did, kept me from coming forward.

"From the moment I left your father, I concluded I'd regret my actions for the rest of my life, and I have. We can't change the past, but I hope you forgive me. I'll forever treasure you in my heart."

Travis wiped the tears off her face.

Sabrina continued. "Your father's a good man. I lacked conviction. Life with your father ended when he converted to Christianity.

"After I left, I moved often. I made it hard on your father to find me. I left you behind because you deserved better. Your life's valuable to me. To drag you along to who knows where is unhealthy and cruel for a child."

Stunned by the revelation, Travis hugged her and said, "I'm sorry that no one informed you, and I hate to be the bearer of unpleasant news. Dad passed away five years ago."

She appeared shaken by the news, and her hands trembled. "I didn't hear Alfredo had passed." Sorrow mapped his mother's face.

Travis led her by the arm and said, "Come into my

office, Mom.

We'll share our experiences and get reacquainted."

Travis advised his secretary, "Take a message if anyone calls."

"I'm leaving back to New York tomorrow," Sabrina said. "I'm glad we've talked, son. Undoubtedly, the Lord's eyes were on you from the start. The image of when you prayed with your tiny little hands clasped before the Lord is vivid in my mind."

Travis's mother lived a complicated life. Sabrina's features had changed, and Travis first fell short of recognizing her. Her hair had turned silvery gray, and she limped with anguish. But as he sat close to his mother, discernible features he knew became known.

"Mom," he said. "Precious time has passed, but our love for each other has never died. Would you consider making your home with us?

~*~*~*~

Pearl, and I will regard it as a blessing."

"No, I can't," Sabrina said, her voice trembling with regret, "but thank you for the offer—
New York's my home. I belong there. But before I leave, I must ask for your forgiveness for abandoning you at such a tender age."

"Yes, I forgive you," he said, his voice filled with relief and joy. Travis hugged her tightly and kissed her forehead. "I missed you, Mom."

"Please forgive me for placing such a heavy burden on you. Living in confusion brings harm. And my actions hurt your father. The Lord is now my Savior, bringing me peace, and His word has enlightened me.

"The greatest news I've heard in a long time," Travis said.

"I went before the congregation before I came here," she said.

Travis kept shaking his head, unable to speak for a

while. After a minute, he said, "I'm grateful God uses people in such a vital and spiritual way.

"If you stay, I'll treasure the privilege of caring for you, Mom."

"No, I'm going back home to New York. God has equipped me to face whatever the enemy brings my way. I'll tell him my son is a pastor, and he's praying for my welfare. He'll flee."

They both found it amusing.

Travis embraced her. "Yes, the Lord will protect you, but I'll miss you."

Sabrina responded with a sweet smile. "The Lord has reunited us. Now you're duty-bound to visit your mother in New York."

Travis agreed. "Better get ready because we'll soon knock on your front door." Travis paused and added, "May I ask you for a favor before we say goodbye?"

"Yes, what can I help you with, son?"

Travis smiled. Sabrina called him son, and he appreciated it, which brought a sense of belonging. With his mother back in his life, compassion filled his heart for her. "Mom," he said, "Please come and meet my wife and dine with us tonight. I'll take you to the airport tomorrow."

"Yes, I'd love to meet Pearl," Sabrina replied. "She's an amazing person and a blessing. Thank God for giving you a delightful spiritual woman for a mate."

Travis's voice grew softer. He said, "Mom, I'm a wealthy man. I'll be blessed to take care of all your needs. The apartment where we live sits empty and awaits you. We'll care for you if you stay and live with us."

Sabrina smiled and said, "Thank you, son. One room is enough for me. I'm comfortable where I live."

Travis's eyes rested on her, and he said, "From here on, you'll receive a love gift each month." He handed her an envelope.

Sabrina patted his hand. "My son, you're a kind and

generous man, and I thank you. I'll accept your gift."

"If you see a moving van parked in your front yard, we've come for you."

On Friday, Travis heard a low rumble from an approaching storm.

He sat in the Detective's office, waiting to talk to Eagle Eye.

The winter reminds me of a carefree time from long ago with Dad when he added fishing to my summer recreation. A time I'll forever cherish, he thought. Oh, how I wish to enjoy his blessings one more time and receive his advice on this terrible predicament we have with Dino.

Travis ambled to the window of his high-rise office, which offered a panoramic view of the city. The day remained gloomy and disheartening, mirroring his mood.

We need convincing evidence to charge Dino with attempted murder when we apprehend him. Travis thought that for the charge to stick, we must find the vehicle Dino had driven the night before the accident.

Eagle Eye moved with great energy. "If this fails, we'll charge Dino with intimidation, harassment, and intent to kidnap," he said.

"A person's guilt of harassment in the first degree arises when he intends and continues to harass another person and follow them. Or if they behave in a way that causes a victim to fear for their safety."

Eagle Eye continued, "Threats to inflict physical harm or assaults for intentions to frighten, each carry a charge."

"I'd say Dino's guilty," Travis said.

"If we can prove Dino is guilty, Travis said, his voice filled with a mix of determination and concern, 'he will spend his life behind bars. And there are other crimes he's committed. In the meantime, I'll have to get more evidence of the accident.'

'No matter what you learn about the case,' Travis

told the Detective, his voice firm with determination. 'You bring me the details and don't share them with anyone. I'd hate for Pearl to find out and experience a setback.'

Pearl may not manage this well."

"I'm doing the whole enchilada to help you, and Pearl enjoy peace," Eagle Eye said.

~*~*~*~

Eagle Eye called Travis the following day, and Pearl answered the phone. "Good morning. I hope you and Travis are safe."

"There's no choice but to navigate our ship," Pearl said, her voice tinged with fear, "but I'm still afraid of the inevitable storm."

"I'm sorry. I don't have good news, but I will work as fast as possible. As for Dino, I'm sure he went into hiding.

Tell Travis to call for help and not to take him on alone if he runs into him."

"You will not capture Dino without a fight," Pearl said.

"If he's looking for a fight, a fight he'll get," Eagle Eye declared with unwavering resolve.

"There's a problem; Dino doesn't fight fair."

"Hard to imagine he'll want to fight, Travis."

"I'm not worried about a fight, but on the weapon he might use."

"Honey, take every precaution necessary. I need to talk to Travis."

"I'll have him return your call," Pearl said.

Minutes later, Travis called Eagle Eye, "Sorry I missed your call."

"I didn't mention it to you," he said. "I plan to review Dino's records in Genoa on Monday and might need your help."

"There's a problem with your call for help. My answer depends on Pearl. I can't leave her alone. Pearl formed a frown.

"I'll have one of my female detectives stay with her."

~*~*~*~

After two days on the job, Eagle Eye and Travis stopped and rested.

"After probing Dino's past, we have found no proof of any illegal activities. Someone here must keep Dino's criminal record clean."

"These people watch out for Dino's interests and keep him well informed," Travis said.

"We ought to abandon the hope of finding evidence against Dino."

When they started their investigation, they met an unsolved crime that disturbed them."

Travis listened with extreme interest as the Detective explained the case. "This young woman went missing two years back. A home builder excavated his property to build his home at the edge of a mountain and discovered bone fragments. The builder turned them in for investigation. These bone fragments found a well-known woman, thanks to DNA."

Someone killed this woman. They killed her, burned her body, and buried her bone fragments. They abandoned the case, and the authorities charged no one with her murder. The issue is still open."

"How horrific," Travis said. "Can we use this evidence against Dino?"

"I'll admit we can't trace the homicide back to Dino. But I have a strong hunch the Mafioso has taken part."

"Someone must know what happened to her. "We need to find this terrible person who executed this horrendous crime," Eagle Eye said.

~*~*~*~

The following morning, the conversation about the specific fragments found at the crime scene continued. "I

stayed awake until midnight studying this case. Eagle Eye
said we don't know who's involved, but the woman lived
with Dino before disappearing. I've decided to unravel this
mystery. And when it happens, we may have enough
evidence from these fragments to pin the murder on him."

"Records show Dino's still a person of interest for a
time.

The Italian investigators, who initially had the
opportunity to link Dino to the murder,
messed up. They lack interest and don't care to pursue this
case. Dino had the opportunity and the motive to commit
the crime and show what may have influenced him."

"What's the motive?" Travis asked.

"The rumors around the police department say she
had left him. People say they see her from time to time.
One day, she vanished. This case shows no arrests have
taken place. The story gets even stranger. No one ever
reported this young woman missing.

"This concerns me. We lack evidence to link Dino
to this crime. But we hope someone knows what happened
and will divulge information," he said and paused.

"I'm disappointed by the lack of cooperation I've
received from these individuals here. People get nervous
when someone questions them about this woman. I'm sure
everyone recalls, but they can't remember the details.
Know what I mean?"

"It doesn't surprise me," Travis said. "Dino's a
violent man, and people worry about retaliation."

"I agree with you. People sometimes deny any
knowledge of Dino. In comparison, others refrain from
talking for fear of getting involved.

"Lupe, a woman in her late fifties who rented out
rooms at the time, offered information. She said her friend
Bella intended to rent a room from her, but Dino
discovered the plan and stopped her," Eagle Eye said.

"They killed my friend Bella Moreno," Lupe said.

"If you continue to snoop around here, someone you least expect will stab you in the back."

Lupe continued. "Dino tried to intimidate the town officials into dropping the investigation on Bella. Not sure if he persuaded them. I know the person who killed my friend, but I lack proof. This organization warned anyone suspected of cooperating with the law would pay with their life."

"This lady warned us to get out of town."

"Again, what is the name of the victim?" Travis enquired.

"Moreno," Eagle Eye said.

"I find the mentioning Pearl's family name in this report odd. A coincidence?"

"Interesting. I didn't think of that," Eagle Eye remarked.

That evening, Travis contacted Pearl from the dimly lit room. "Hi, honey. I called to check on you."

"The neighborhood is quiet," Pearl replied, "but I miss you."

"Yes, and I miss you, too."

"How's the company?"

"Oh, she's fantastic."

"You two get along well?"

"Yes, she's an interesting woman."

"Don't take unnecessary chances," he warned, his voice laced with worry. "Need you to promise me you'll stay home. Stay put."

"I don't plan to leave the apartment. Please hurry home. I sense Dino's prowling around here," she whispered, her voice trembling with fear.

"No problem, we've finished here. We'll be heading home. The minute we arrived here, the Detective started on this case."

"Find any evidence you can use against Dino?" Pearl asked.

"We found out someone dropped a case before they solved it.

"Eagle Eye intends to investigate the cause of the case's dismissal. But we have no evidence against Dino. Eagle Eye plans to use scary tactics to arouse fear. We may get Dino to confess his crimes against you."

"What's the plan?" Pearl wanted to know.

"We'll convince him we have a witness to testify against him. Dino must respond, and if we're successful, he'll confess," Travis said, his voice filled with determination.

"Dino's a clever man and won't fall for it. He'll want proof," Pearl said. "But with his position with mafia members, he might've ordered it done."

"We have to rattle his brain and make him nervous."

"I forewarned you. Dino is a wise man. He'll elude the local law enforcement. Dino might employ a double."

"You may have unveiled a clue. It never entered my mind. It'll be an immense problem, and Dino might outsmart the law again."

"The circumstances with Dino scare me, but I'm at peace when you're home."

Travis prayed, "God, guard Pearl's heart and mind and let my words be sufficient with grace. Travis paused for a moment. "Honey," he asked, "what's your mother's full name?"

"Dad called her Belle Rose, but her name is Bella Moreno."

After another pause, Travis asked, "Honey, what happened to your mother?"

"Mom ran off with another man. Why do you ask?"

Travis gave a dubious explanation. "Oh, for most of the day, my thoughts rested on you," he said, his voice filled with curiosity and concern, "I questioned if your mother's as cordial and charming as you. I can't help but wonder about the woman who raised you."

"Strange, you asked," Pearl said, her voice filled with sadness and determination. "Her memory lingered in my mind all day. I plan to ask her why she left without me when I find her. I wonder if she's still as beautiful and kind as I remember. That's if I find her."

"Who knows? She might be in a predicament beyond her control. Help me, Lord," he prayed.

"Travis, have you located my mother in Genoa?"

"No, sweetheart, the detective is calling. When I get in this evening, we'll talk about it."

"I'll see you when you get home," she said in a whisper.

"Unbelievable," Travis said. "The same predator who victimized Pearl might've killed Pearl's mother. It makes me nauseous to think he may have violated this family twice."

"I've said it before the man's appalling. He has no limits, said the detective."

When the detective and Travis left Genoa, the status of this murder case stayed the same: unsolved.

Late afternoon, Pearl asked Travis, "Honey, I hate to put you in this position. I'm not forcing you to lie, but I must ask. Is my mother dead? Please tell me the truth. I need to reckon with my mother's death.

"You need to ask Eagle Eye. I don't have answers for you."

"Oh, my dear Lord, you've answered my question," she said. "I feared someone might kill her before I found her. They've killed my beloved mother," she said, weeping.

Travis looked into his wife's tear-filled eyes and said, "Honey, I'm sorry, your guess is as good as mine. Please trust me. I didn't uncover any proof to support your suspicions. I wish we'd gathered more details. Eagle Eye will have to answer your questions."

Travis knew his answer to her question needed more substance.

"From the depths of my shattered soul, I know my mother's dead," she said, and tears, heavy with grief, rolled down her cheeks.

"You're a compassionate man. But life is unfair. I hope you didn't withhold information. It's the answer I must accept for now. I suppose I'll hear the complete story in the future," she said, her voice tinged with a hint of suspicion.

"Honey, I'm sorry," he said, pulling her closer.

CHAPTER 12~DANGER AT HOME

La Spezia.

Travis asked Pearl if she was getting ready to join him this Friday morning.

"Honey, what's the plan today?"

Pearl smiled. "I take pleasure in staying home on Friday mornings. I plan to clean the apartment today."

"You're sure you want to stay home today?"

"I'm a big girl. I'm fine."

"Is anxiety getting better?"

"My fears haven't changed," she said, dismissing the topic. "I must remove these books from the front room."

"Okay, call me if you need me."

Minutes after Travis left for work, Pearl became edgy. Her eyes were big and wide, and anxiety filled her heart. She glanced into the bedroom.

"Lord, strengthen me," she prayed.

"The thought of someone else besides me inside this apartment makes me tremble in fear. Lord, it's my first time alone in days."

Pearl strolled down the hall toward the other bedroom and advanced to the living room window. Pearl paused for a quick breath and moved to the large double doors leading to the patio.

"Lord, I have the jitters. This feeling has taken control of my nerves. It's a weird experience to find yourself alone. The noises heard can cause paranoia.

"Calm my heart, Lord," she prayed. She stroked her hair back over her ear and returned to her work. Minutes later, she whispered, "I can't shake this sense of imminent danger that has come over me."

"It's as if I'm expecting danger. But there's no reason to consider it a threat."

Pearl heard a thump. "I fear the unknown," she whispered. She listened, and she heard another thump. "My heart's throbbing. No, the noise came from outside or from the kitchen." Pearl shivered.

She made her way around the corner and peeked into the kitchen. And Dino stood there by the cabinets. Dino entered and crept inside like a cockroach. Travis neglected to lock the kitchen door when he left.

Pearl let out a blood-curdling scream, and her entire body froze. Dino rushed with a knife he'd taken from the drawer. It caused her to burst into tears. He smiled and made the scar on his upper lip more noticeable.

Dino grabbed her by the shoulders and shook her. "Keep quiet if you want to live."

She ended her struggle. The pain in her shoulder radiated to her head.

She asked him, "How did you get in?"

"Oh, Amore," Dino said, shrugging. "I have trouble resisting unlocked doors. I take advantage of the mistakes others make."

Pearl continued to weep in silence. "Get out!" she screamed.

Dino held her tight by the shoulders. "Come with me," he said, kissing her forehead.

Pearl fought him off and backed away. Dino made a quick move and grabbed her arm.

"What makes you assume I'll go anywhere with you? I'd rather die first than go with you. Kill me and bring this nightmare to an end."

He said calmly and arrogantly, "Well, if you insist, you may leave us sooner than planned."

Pearl's gut tightened with despair. "Why can't you let me live my life? I worked hard for you, but free labor's over." For a brief time, Dino's grip gave way to her plea. "If you come with me without a struggle, I won't harm you or Travis."

Pearl feared for Travis. "Travis will return in a matter of minutes.

He will not stand by and watch while you take me away."

"If you don't shut your mouth and come with me, I'll sit here and wait for your precious Travis. When we leave, Travis will no longer be a problem."

Pearl recognized that Dino meant every word he uttered. She mustered enough courage to elbow him. Dino's breath left his body in a whoosh. His head snapped back, and he reeled off balance. Dino steadied himself and slapped her.

"I'll go with you, but you must promise you won't harm Travis."

"Dino frowned."

She heard her subconscious say. "Don't trust Dino." The words pounded in her head.

Someone once said, "When he speaks, believe him not, for there are seven abominations in his heart."

Hostility masked Dino's face. "Harm him?" he said. "I gave my men orders to kill him last time. I won't make the same mistake. Now let's go!"

Pearl held a place card that slipped from her hand when Dino first lunged at her. Dino noticed what occupied her time before he entered. Dino picked up the card from the floor. "Oh, how sweet."

Pearl ignored his observation.

"Sorry, I didn't attend your grand celebration. But a busy day kept me away. Busy creating a plan to rescue you from Travis.

The wedding ceremony is of no importance. You're still mine."

Pearl broke loose and ran for her life. Seconds away

from the door, Dino grabbed her left arm, which he held in an iron grip. "If any other woman ever played games with my heart like you, she'd die on the spot. Time to teach you a lesson you'll remember for a long time," Dino said.

"Let's go. Walk out the door without drawing attention from neighbors. Be smart or pay a hefty price."

Pearl dragged her foot, caught the edge of a rug, and fell.

"You klutz," he said. He reached and yanked her to her feet.

Dino experienced an excellent fall and injured his pride. Pearl grabbed his arm and threw him off-kilter, but he fell near the fireplace. Hatred burned within the depths of his soul. He scrambled to his feet.

"There're consequences for mistakes, and you'll pay for yours," he said. "Now, walk out the door."

~*~*~*~

Travis called to check on Pearl, but there was no answer.

"I'm going home, I'm worried for Pearl," Travis told Eagle Eye. "The news of her mother dampened her spirit. When he pushed open the unlocked door, he knew from the silence that Pearl had faced danger. Silence contributes to an effective form of communication, he thought.

"What I feared the most has happened." The question of Pearl's whereabouts sent profound hysteria through his entire body.

Travis checked the other rooms. He felt defeated as he took small, measured steps back to the front room. He wanted to run out the door and scream for help, but his body didn't obey his command.

He prayed in silence. Father, we're troubled yet not distressed.

Perplexed, but not in despair, for in You, we're strong.

"Pearl, answer me," he whispered. It hit Travis like a

wave of emotion. In sickness and in health, till death do us part.

The unbreakable promise they'd agreed to keep. A great fear came over Travis, and they called Joe. "I have a gut feeling that terror has invaded our home. Pearl's not here, and she's not answering her phone. I believe she's in danger. I must find her before Dino takes her to another country."

"She must have stepped out," Joe said.

"No, she fears Dino. I know he's kidnapped her. He'll kill her."

The voices in Travis's head warned him, 'Be strong. Be courageous. Do not fear him.' But terror crept through him like slow-acting venom. I must play it smart and not panic to make the right decisions.

"Lord, please protect Pearl," he prayed.

Joe dropped what he was doing and joined his friend.

Travis appeared worse than Joe had thought.

"Have you called the police?"

"Pearl's gone," Travis said, his voice above a whisper. He looked bewildered.

Joe turned around to see sorrow flood his friend's eyes. A worried frown had claimed his face. "Don't imagine the worst. We'll find her," Joe said.

"I'm sorry. I can't control myself, but I'm worried sick. There's no way to get Dino to stop this madness."

"Stay here," Joe said. "I'll come back in a few minutes."

"I'll go with you."

But the detective's car came into sight.

Travis responded the moment he spotted Eagle Eye and hurried to meet him.

"How did you find out?"

"Find out about what?" The detective asked, holding on to his attached case.

"Dino took Pearl!"

"What do you mean he took Pearl?"

"He kidnapped her."

The detective stared at Travis without blinking. A challenge appeared on his impassive face. He recognized how grave this may get.

He understood the need and the time he had to stop this weird man from committing a fatal crime.

The unpredictability of this news caused a second pulse to throb beneath his skin.

Travis stared at him with an intense look, his face motionless.

The detective's face softened. "I'm sorry," he said.

"We must find Pearl before he takes her out of the country. I should've stayed home today." Travis vented his fears. "How is it possible Dino entered the house?"

"We must place Dino's estate on twenty-four-hour surveillance," the detective said.

Travis raised his hands in the air. "What can surveillance do?

He's not taking her to his home. It'll be the first place the police will check."

The detective pulled out his phone and didn't waste time calling his partner. Travis overheard him say. "Get ready to turn this town upside down."

Travis heard him say, "The terrorist organizations get their funds by kidnapping young girls."

"An educated guess," Eagle Eye said. "These gang members make more than five hundred million dollars a year in ransom payments."

Unaware that Travis heard every word, the detective continued, "We must act fast. Dino's a killer."

Travis winced in fear. His dark hair fell over his brow. Without hesitation, he ran his hand through his hair, revealing his anguish.

"Eliminating a few scenarios will help," Eagle Eye

said. He dusted off his buckskin pants and pulled his slouch hat closer to his eyes. He blocked the sun's glare, peeking through the trees, and continued with questions.

While they stood outside in a group discussion, a neighbor came over to offer his knowledge of the kidnap. This chap removed his wide-brim hat, scratched his head, and said, "A rusty black truck came by and left with the young lady. She appeared reluctant to go with him. He used force by pulling her to the truck."

"When people offer their observations, a case is easier to solve," Eagle Eye said, thanks to everyone here. Keep your eyes open and call me with any latest information the minute you hear it," Eagle Eye said. He gave them his business card.

Another gentleman came forward. "I saw a strange sight today," Miguel said. "A man walked right into this house. Someone must've left the door unlocked."

"How's it possible?" Eagle Eyes asked.

"I live across the street. The house is visible from my kitchen. I'm telling you, this man walked in without knocking.

"Did you call and report this to the police?" the detective asked.

"No. We saw this truck days ago. The driver wanted people to notice him because he stopped in the street. We thought he had come to steal our tools. Thieves get our attention in this neighborhood. We have a way of taking care of them ourselves. We had prepared to deal with him today if he came back."

"I thank you; this information has helped," Eagle Eye said.

The Italian police stepped over to talk to a group of curious neighbors who had gathered in the front yard.

From a neighbor, Travis overheard. Victims who vanish are occasionally kidnapped and held against their will in exchange for a ransom. If they don't get paid, they either torture or murder them.

Travis heard another neighbor say. "A murderer will hide the corpse and dispose of it to escape discovery. So, the person killed vanishes without a trace." His head throbbed, and his stomach turned.

He stormed off to avoid the gossip. After realizing he hadn't locked the door, Travis climbed into his truck to search for Pearl.

"How can I forgive myself for such carelessness? I'm sorry, Pearl, for putting you through such a terrifying ordeal.

"I'll make the airport my first stop before a shift change and check the flights to Rome. by surprise."

"How can I forgive myself for such carelessness? I'm sorry, Pearl, for putting you through such a terrifying ordeal.

"I'll make the airport my first stop before a shift change and check the flights to Rome. I'll ask if anyone has seen Pearl with Dino.

"Dino's on a winning streak. It's not long before he makes a mistake. It's a matter of time."

The morning after, Travis noticed the detective's face, etched with concern and with an exhausted appearance. "'Travis, you look dreadful. Did you manage to get any sleep last night?'"

"Not a wink."

"Call the doctor," he said. "He'll give you a sedative to relax."

"No thanks, hard to work with drugs running through my system."

"Travis, you need your sleep. You must stay alert during the day. Pay careful attention to what you say. Someone in the police department's administration office keeps Dino informed."

"And where does it leave us?"

"Good question. Sensitive information is not the

first time it gets into the public. I don't have a clue whom to trust."

"The longer it takes to capture Dino, the greater the danger for Pearl," Travis said.

"For Pearl and us," Travis heard the detective say.

We pray You will shine Your light on us and get us out of this darkness and fear, Travis prayed.

He set off to meet the detective, his mind swirling with questions. "Will Dino whisk her away to Rome? Is Pearl in Genoa, and is she still breathing? I must find her before a catastrophic event unfolds.

The authorities thrust Pearl into the center of an intense overnight search, a search born out of the fear and dread that Dino's notorious reputation instilled.

We pray You will shine Your light on us and get us out of this darkness and fear, Travis prayed.

He set off to meet the detective, his mind swirling with a multitude of questions. "Will Dino whisk her away to Rome? Is Pearl in Genoa, and is she still breathing? I must find her before a catastrophic event unfolds."

"Where has Dino taken Pearl?" Travis wondered.

"Dino has relatives in Florence, Eagle Eye said. This information comes from his records. He owns property on the outskirts of town, where he entertains his girlfriends and stores his boat and other heavy equipment. This hideaway exists someplace toward the mountains."

"You must be specific, don't guess?" We'll waste time, and men will die if we make mistakes," Travis said.

~*~*~*~

Dino yanked Pearl before dawn the following day and dragged her back to the truck.

He tied her to a tire rim. "I suppose you wonder why we're taking the side roads." Pearl kept her eyes closed to avoid the sun's glare, reflecting from the tire rim, causing significant discomfort.

Dino had tormented her throughout this journey. He intended to kill her, but when and where?

"Say goodbye to Genoa and Travis," Dino announced.

Pearl opened her eyes wide. He still plans to kill Travis. Or has my demise arrived? "Oh Lord, save us from this madman," she prayed. Pearl's fear escalated and obstructed her airway. Breathing had become difficult.

Dino drove to a restaurant and threw a cover over Pearl. He left her in the hot truck while he ate a tasty, warm breakfast. Dino bought an egg sandwich for Pearl, which she refused to eat. After scolding her for not eating, he drove to a park and left Pearl alone. He strolled to a post office and sent Travis a packet.

When Dino returned, Pearl appeared on the verge of passing out. He ran his fingers across her face and said, "The temperature's hot today, huh?"

Dino hummed the tune of his favorite song, *Forever Mine*. Get comfortable before we take off to the next town.

I'll follow his orders to stall, she thought.

Her leg slipped, and she booted him, bringing him to his knees.

The incident angered him. He reached for a bungee cord, whacked Pearl's legs, and continued to hit her body. Dino notices an elderly couple in the park focused on his brutal act.

"Those old people ought to mind their own business." He struggled to tie Pearl to the steel rim, jumped in the truck, and rushed through traffic.

The stunning couple reported Dino's cruel actions to the police.

~*~*~*~

Dino had planned to spend the night in a small town. The afternoon arrived, and Dino appeared spooked.

Whether Dino received information from a reliable source or had a strange feeling after making a phone call, he said, "I've changed my plans. Let's hit the road."

He drove awhile and said, "I have to find a secluded place to park this truck." He scrambled to the back a minute later and yanked the truck door open.

"Hurry," he yelled. "It's time to catch a flight."

Pearl awaited Dino to untie her. The end has arrived for me, she thought.

Dino noticed her nervousness. "Oh no, Amore, this is not the climax. I have a special surprise in mind for you."

Pearl's actions and her trembling showed her genuine feelings.

"If the folks in the park call the police authorities, and they come looking for us, they'll find an empty truck. I've planned this for a long time and want this journey drawn out in hopes you'll enjoy it."

The hum of a helicopter approaching from the west disrupted her thoughts. "Time to abandon the truck. We'll try my chopper next."

The helicopter hovered about a hundred yards from where they waited.

Dino pulled Pearl's gag off, and she gasped for air. Dino shouted above the roar of the chopper. "Duck your head if you don't want to lose it."

Pearl stumbled and fell.

"Get to your feet, or I'll leave you here."

Dino reached out, yanked Pearl to her feet, and pushed her into the helicopter.

Dino stretched to see the ground as they flew over the city. "The pilot will make a quick stop to fuel at Monaco Airport," he said.

"I'm warning you not to instigate any trouble if you don't want to see Travis get what he deserves. I'm still in contact with my men. And you, Missy, will plead with me to finish with you," he smiled.

Dino's a man who instills the fear of manipulation, she thought.

"Your plans are of little importance," she said. "And what you say amounts to empty words to me."

This remark irritated him, and he slapped her.

The pilot announced he'd make an immediate stop to fuel.

As the chopper landed, Dino kept his hand over Pearl's mouth until he gave her instructions.

"Don't scream. Cooperate with me. Travis is within my reach."

I'll keep my lips taut and clamped shut. Dino means every word he spews out of his mouth.

Lord, I have various regrets and resentments for my mother, who left me behind with Dad. The most debilitating part of my life was when I escaped and met Dino, the devil. I ought to have stayed home and reasoned with Dad. These regrets have turned my soul toxic toward Dino.

Dino looked content as he surveyed the terrain from the helicopter. "The pilot will stop at Malaga Airport," he said, smiling. "From Malaga Airport, we'll go to Algarve Airport in Portugal. Travis won't find you there. He'll get confused and admit defeat if he tries to follow our trail."

Dino stared at Pearl. "I hope you'll enjoy the flight," he said. But his gentleness lasted a brief time. He became unhinged when the chopper landed. "Where's my gun?" he shouted. "I must've left it in the truck or lost my weapon at Monaco when I stepped out. Turn around and go back."

"Don't worry, boss," the pilot said. "I'll go buy another gun when we land in Algarve. I'll take care of your gun on the way back. Relax and enjoy yourself while you're here."

"Relax!" Dino yelled. "Who needs to relax? They'll find my fingerprints on the gun. Go back!"

"No," the pilot said. "Different brands of weapons await you in Algarve. I'll have someone in Genoa retrieve your gun from the truck."

Minutes later, Dino drove a car his pilot rented. On

the way to a quiet motel, he changed his mind and rented an inexpensive motel.

Dino looked pleased with the new handgun the pilot bought, symbolizing his power and control in this foreign land.

He spat and wiped the gun clean with his spit.

"While we're here in Portugal," Dino said, "we'll catch up on our swimming. And we'll go scuba diving in one of the best spots in Portugal."

"If you decide not to join me, I must tie you to the bed."

"A sign on the door will tell the house cleaners we're busy, and they'll bypass the room. I plan to enjoy myself here and suggest you do the same."

Dino's eyes darted around the room. "Not too shabby," he said, his voice laced with a hint of uncertainty. "We may stay here for a while. Better get used to the place," he told Pearl, the air thick with an unspoken threat.

Who will question his business in Algarve? She thought. Her mind was a whirlwind of fear and uncertainty. He'll enjoy his stay without fear of interference from the local authorities. And he'll celebrate without worrying while I grow weaker by the day, her inner turmoil growing with each passing moment.

~*~*~*~

Back home, Travis and Joe stayed busy, seeking clues. We need more information on Dino's recent activities.

"I'm convinced Dino stayed closer to us in more ways than one," Travis said.

"A man named Bruno is in jail waiting for sentencing for an assault case on an officer," Eagle Eye said.

"This attack happened in Dino's neighborhood. Please find out how this individual linked himself to Dino. He's known for doing odd jobs for the mafia, which might include murder," Eagle Eye said.

"Bruno's known as being a sympathizer to mafia groups in Italy. It might help you if you consider what he admits is false. Gather information, and we'll try to make sense of his story."

Before Bruno appeared, Joe paced the floor in this local jail hall.

Bruno rounded his torso and wrapped his arms around his stomach when he walked.

"You have bruised ribs?" Joe asked.

Bruno ignored Joe and coughed.

"I demand answers, Bruno," Joe said, his voice laced with authority. "And if your responses fail to satisfy me, you'll yearn for a glimpse of the sun."

"I have nothing to hide," he said.

"Good to know you'll be honest."

"When the police brutalized me, life blurred into a haze. Life's cruel and empty, like a fading dream," Bruno confessed, his voice tinged with pain.

"This beating has hurt me physically and psychologically."

"Sorry, I can't help you," Joe said. "I'm here to gather information on your associates. I hope we can work as partners."

"What associates?"

"The ones you rely on for work."

Bruno nodded and squirmed.

"What's your full name?" Joe asked.

"My name is Bruno Mancini. I live without hope of belonging to any country."

"If this self-pity behavior continues, it's going to drag you into depression," Joe said.

"It's easy for you to say. You're not the one suffering and having to answer questions," Bruno said, his voice trembling with a mix of fear and anger. The interrogation was taking a toll on him, and Joe could see that.

"Expressing sorrow or despair will not help," Joe replied and continued. "Name your last employer?"

"I was born, raised, and worked in Florence, and I forgot the name of my employer. You're not getting any more information from me." He raised his hands in a rebellious way.

"If you persist in this resistance, I can't assist in your release," Joe declared, his determination unwavering. He continued to press Bruno, unrelenting in his interrogation.

"Where's your home these days?"

"I stay at the Hostel Genoa when I'm in town. A new boarding house in the city," he said.

"Is Dino your childhood friend?"

Bruno frowned and rolled his eyes. "I can't remember."

"Do you use or sell drugs?"

Bruno ignored his question and started coughing.

Joe gave him a stern look and asked. "Tell me if Dino's an acquaintance or your business partner?"

Bruno hesitated, then finally spoke. "I'm acquainted with him, but he's not a nice man to befriend."

"What other work identifies you with him, other than dealing drugs?" Joe asked in a severe tone.

Joe lifted his eyebrows. "Okay, we can make progress," he said.

"Clarify your duties when you worked for Dino. And have you distributed drugs for him?"

Bruno's demeanor altered, and he struggled to change his answer.

After he scowled at his challenger, he added, "No, I never worked for him. I meant he's a customer of mine in the barbershop."

"I'll ask you again, and I want a truthful answer," Joe said.

"When you work for Dino, name your duties?"

Bruno gave him a sheepish grin and turned hostile. "I have the privilege of refusing to answer your questions."

"Of course, you do," Joe said, "but it'll be helpful if you cooperate."

"I have no secrets," he said. "My life, as I recall, is an open book, and I have done no wrong."

"The police authorities charged you with assaulting an officer. What are your answers?"

"You misunderstood," he said. He coughed and wrapped his arms around his torso. "The police assaulted me."

"As your friend, I'm warning you, better cooperate with me. Tell me, how long have you worked for Dino?"

"My dealings with Dino are favors. Stop trying to inflict injustice with what I do in life."

"I need detailed information on your friend Dino. I'll leave you alone If you can give me the information."

"Bruno, a suspect in our ongoing investigation, claimed they were merely 'favors," Bruno said, referring to the illicit activities we suspect him of.

"What's the most unworthy plea one can receive from a friend when they need or ask for a favor? A favor differs because the person's crafty enough to plead to your soft side. "They promised to return the favor, but they cannot keep their promise," Joe said.

Bruno's smile seemed forced. "I find many fun ways to make extra money on the side," he said, his voice betraying his nervousness. "You can't blame a guy for bettering himself, right?"

"Did Dino pay you for favors? And what do you call favors? One who steals commits a criminal offense. Dealing with drugs is a crime. Get my drift?"

"What do you want from me?" Bruno asked.

"I've told you, Bruno, I want the truth. I know you lie as you breathe. The law locked you up because you have committed a crime," Joe said, his voice firm and steady.

Joe wrinkled one brow. "Let me explain the truth in a simple term. The truth's the actual state of the matter. Earlier, you told me you collaborated with Dino. Now you tell me you carried out favors for him. Which one's the truth?"

"I misunderstood your question," Bruno said.

"You mean you lied on purpose? Remember why you're in jail and on the way to prison?"

"You're being unfair to how you treat me," he whined.

"I've treated you better than you deserve.

"Bruno, you've tried to harm people with no remorse.

You gave me a fictitious location and claimed you'd done no business with Dino when it's clear you've worked together. You've lied to me the entire time.

"Let's answer at least one question with the truth. Who's your boss now?"

Bruno appeared evasive.

"Okay," Joe said. "We'll have to transfer you from Genoa to Florence's jail."

"I want to stay in Genoa." Bruno frowned and looked fearful.

"You have no choice. I can promise you that Florence is looking forward to seeing you. I intended to help you stay here, but you won't cooperate."

Bruno pleaded. "I'll give you the information if you help me stay here in Genoa."

Joe smiled. "Does a secret threat await you in Florence that you fear facing?"

"No," he said, frowning in disapproval.

A satisfied smile appeared on Joe's face. "Okay, start talking and tell the truth this time."

"I often come to Genoa from Florence and mend what's broken. Those are favors for Dino," he explained, his voice calm and steady.

"I've had it with your lies," Joe said, his voice filled with frustration. "You've stuck to the same answers and made your choice," he added, his disappointment clear as he turned and walked out of the room.

~*~*~*~

In the detective's office in La Spezia, Joe, a seasoned detective, met with Travis, a young and eager officer, and Eagle Eye, a skilled investigator, to compare notes. "Bruno's a depraved individual," Joe said, his voice filled with conviction.

"My interrogation didn't get answers for you, so I acted at another level. To my surprise, I learned Dino patronizes Bruno's barbershop."

"It's obvious he's made himself available for Dino with gusto," Travis said.

"I've learned Bruno hangs around Dino and his cronies. He must know how Dino works," Eagle Eye said, his voice filled with determination. "A clever idea comes to mind. We must collect evidence on Dino and Bruno, and we must do it now."

"Bruno won't cause us any more problems if he's found guilty," the detective said. "He'll spend years behind bars for an assault on an officer. He has a long rap sheet. They might ship him back to Florence. Who knows what his future holds? The sentence he'll get and where they'll send him to serve his sentence is unknown."

"If you've injured an officer, it's a proven fact that you'll serve time."

~*~*~*~

Mid-morning came around when the mail carrier delivered a packet to Travis with no return address.

"I hope this sheds light on Pearl's location," he whispered.

Travis opened the envelope. "This is an old article dated months ago in Genoa. It details a woman who mysteriously vanished in the depths of the Mediterranean Sea," he whispered, his voice filled with a mix of intrigue and concern.

The headline read: "Local Woman Lost at Sea."

"What does this mean? Lord, have mercy on us," Travis whispered.

The coastguard found Dino's boat capsized the following day after the accident. The vicious storm that hit Genoa on Thursday afternoon caused this event. Travis read the entire article, his heart sinking with each word.

An intensive search in a fifty-mile radius resulted in the Coast Guard not finding anybody. Law enforcement didn't rule out foul play and detained Dino, among others, as a person of interest.

"Bruno won't cause us any more problems if he's found guilty," the detective said. "He'll spend years behind bars for an assault on an officer. He has a long rap sheet. They might ship him back to Florence. Who knows what his future holds? The sentence he'll get and where they'll send him to serve his sentence is unknown."

"If you've injured an officer, it's a proven fact that you'll serve time."

~*~*~*~

Mid-morning came around when the mail carrier delivered a packet to Travis with no return address.

"I hope this sheds light on Pearl's location," he whispered, his voice filled with a mix of hope and desperation.

Travis, his curiosity piqued, cautiously opened the envelope. "This is an ancient article, a relic from months ago in Genoa. It unveils the tragic tale of a woman who met her watery grave in the Mediterranean Sea," he whispered.

The headline read: "Local Woman Lost at Sea."

"What could this signify? Lord, have mercy on us," he muttered, his voice trembling with uncertainty.

The coastguard found Dino's boat capsized on the day of the accident. The vicious storm that hit Genoa on Thursday afternoon, a storm that was said to be the worst in a decade, caused this event. Travis read the entire article, his mind racing with questions.

An intensive search in a fifty-mile radius ended when the authorities found no bodies. Their brows furrowed with concern; law enforcement didn't rule out foul play and detained Dino, among others, as a person of interest.

CHAPTER 13~THE CHASE

In the meantime, Eagle Eye decided Joe must revisit Bruno in the hopes that he would get helpful information this time.

Joe confronted Bruno and offered his hand for a shake, as he had with a longtime friend.

"How's my big guy?" Joe asked. "I hope they've treated you with respect in this place."

Bruno pumped Joe's hand four or five times, stepped back from the visitor's window, and began with his complaints.

"Money is a problem every man struggles with before they join the mafia. But I learned the organization doesn't care or value lives."

"Oh yeah, what's the problem, my friend?" Joe asked.

Bruno scratched his head and said, "Man, life is tough here."

Joe stared at him, hoping he'd receive specific information on Dino. He picked precise words to communicate with him.

"I earn extra money when I work odd jobs for Dino," Bruno said. "But the last few times, he's treated me with disrespect. Dino does not deliver."

"What do you mean?"

"I've called Dino twice, and he doesn't answer my call. When the time arrives to pay his men for services made, he's not available. Dino doesn't care what happens to his men. He's betrayed me twice."

"I warned you," Joe said. "Where does Dino live nowadays?"

"Dino's place has a for-sale sign, and he's in Portugal."

"Wow, a life of leisure," Joe said.

"Before pleasure can happen, Dino must take care of business."

"Yeah, right, I'm sure. Fishing and scuba diving come to mind," Joe said and smiled.

"No, I'm serious."

"Sorry to hear."

"Dino's teaching his girlfriend a lesson she won't forget."

"How to swim?" Joe asked and laughed.

"This girl's life depends on how well she follows orders," Bruno said, and his eyes narrowed. "Can you post bail for me?"

"I'm sorry, but I have no power here. But do you want to share more information about your group?"

"What group?"

"This must be a case of misinterpretation. I thought you said you belonged to the mafia."

"Oh, yeah, but what's in it for me?"

"I explained how we must follow the rules the last time we met."

Bruno looked around and lowered his voice. "Valuable information seldom comes my way. But I can share details on Dino."

"Well, if the information brings excellent results, I'll talk to someone on your behalf," Joe said.

"Dino purchased a boat," Bruno blurted out.

"A new or used boat?"

"Not sure."

"So, he has a boat. What other information can you contribute?" Bruno glanced around and said, "He bought the boat in Portugal and planned to use it to complete his mission."

"Give me valuable information, and don't waste my time. What's the urgent need for a boat in Portugal?"

"Wait a minute," he said and stepped back. "Will you promise the information I give you will help me, too? I'll release more information when you guarantee me good news."

"Sorry," Joe said. "You're not entitled to choose treatment yet. You haven't given me any information I can use. I can't promise."

Bruno needed to continue begging for bail because of Joe's lack of interest.

"Get me out of here. And I'll fill your ears with valuable information on this organization."

Joe acted uninterested. "It's difficult to convince the head of state to pardon your crime and cancel the penalty due."

Dino changed his mind. "These mafia guys leave no witnesses, and I can name the countries transporting the girls."

"Girls, what girls?" Joe asked.

"The girls sell to whoever has the cash."

"Will you testify against Dino and his men?"

"Yes, I'll testify and give you what you need. Dino will let me rot in jail."

"You know Dino's men well, including your cellmate, right?" Joe asked.

"The ones jailed with me belong to another mafia group. They don't belong to Dino, but they're still mafia. They know what's going on with Dino."

"Let me try this again. You're saying these men can't name you as Dino's man?"

"Complicated, but I hadn't met a group member until I arrived. They don't have anything on me. When Dino wants a small favor done, he calls me. I go back home after I finish the job. We both agree it's best this way. You know what I mean?"

"I'm confused. Can you tell me why you spend time together in Dino's neighborhood? For instance, the day you scuffled with the police."

"I came for payment for another minor job. Dino disappeared before I arrived, which resulted in a brawl with the police and my arrest.

"I know what favors mean to you. Interested in working for the law?" Joe asked.

Bruno made his dislike for officers known with a frown. "Doing what?" he asked.

"It's a minor job, but the officer who charged you with the battery will drop those charges.

You're facing twenty or more years in prison for the officer's offense alone."

"Okay, what's my role?"

"You'll work as an informant."

"But I'll stay jailed?" Bruno whined.

"You'll receive the freedom to move around the grounds. You must report what you hear among the distinct groups to Eagle Eye. And don't show your identity.

"Eagle Eye will receive information from you when he visits you. He's an undercover cop."

"This temporary home in this prison's frigid and gray," Bruno said. "The sick, sad, and broken who suffer here can't recall how freedom feels. They can't recall the trees or flowers. I see them cry through the chilly bars of a cell. But problems will work out."

"Will this job take a while?"

"Let's call it an informant, not a job. The time depends on how fast you'll work. Make friends, and we'll supply the questions you must ask. And cash if you need any."

He hung his head in despair. "I'll try, but if it gets risky, I'll pull out."

"Yes, we'll move you right away. Can I count on

you or not?"

"Yes, I'll try it."

"Expect several visits from Eagle Eye," Joe said.

Bruno's eyes narrowed. "Look, I've given you important information that might get me in trouble."

"Give me a reason why trouble might come."

"When they learn, I've squealed and disclosed secret information about their activities. I'm a dead man."

"Well, you must be smart, my friend. But I still haven't received information concerning the girls."

"I'll release more information after you tell me how long I must commit to doing this dirty job. And how long before I taste freedom?"

"Fair enough," Joe said.

"Has Dino moved to Portugal?"

"Since he put his estate up for sale, no one knows his plans these days?"

"Do you know the young lady he plans to discipline?"

Joe looked at the big man and added, "Thank you, my friend. I'm impressed that you'll risk your life to help the authorities. There's still hope for you."

The minute Joe stepped out of Bruno's sight; he called Travis.

"What took you so long?" Travis asked.

"I have important news. Bruno has agreed to testify against Dino. He promised other information if we arranged his release."

"Have you learned where Dino has taken Pearl?"

"I enjoyed a great session with my friend Bruno today. I plan to honor the promises made. And the information received has significant value."

"Bruno gave us the name of the country where Dino fled with Pearl. If we get the officer to drop the charges against him and get him released, he'll offer more information. We may rescue other young girls before they're trapped with lies and risk death by these sexual predators." Joe said.

~*~*~*~

Two days later, Officer Ortega escorted the detective upstairs to visit Bruno. They found Bruno in the mess hall.

"If you don't mind, give me a minute with Bruno alone," the detective told Officer Ortega. The officer hesitated and moved away with measured steps.

"Hey Bruno, what's the latest?" Eagle Eye asked and sat across from him at the table.

Bruno's eyes darted around the mess hall. "Who sends you here, and what's your business with me?"

"I'm the person you need to trust from here on out. Joe mentioned you're my informant."

"Look, I fear someone will see us talking and incite trouble. I'll drop off my tray and meet you in the hallway."

"Have little time to spare. I'll wait a minute or two, and I'm gone."

Bruno, a fellow inmate in this chaotic prison, followed without delay. "There is pure madness in this prison," he said, his voice barely audible over the din of the crowded hallways.

"How can I persuade you to help me leave this rat place? You're my last chance."

Bruno's eyes darted around the hallway; his voice filled with a chilling warning. "This prison is a living nightmare, a place that devours both guards and inmates alike."

"Life's tough everywhere," Eagle Eye said, hoping to relax him. "And it's a serious circumstance you're facing. We may convince the officer to drop the charges against you. But the information you give me must pan out."

"After I give you the information, can I leave here?"

"You'll have to give us what we need. It may take

time to analyze the information. We'll wait and follow protocol."

Bruno divulged a treasure trove of information, a lifeline to his freedom.

"Don't forget they're flying into Faro Airport and going to Algarve. Dino wants to confuse Travis and stop him from finding Pearl."

"Oh, so Pearl's the name of the girl he wants to control?"

It's a long-time romance gone stale."

~*~*~*~

In the office, Travis and Eagle Eye discussed the sensitive information. "Joe and I must take a jet as soon as possible," Travis said.

"Yes, you must, and I'll stay behind to get Bruno another place if the need arises."

"You must work fast. Bruno wouldn't last a day if he'd discovered it."

"I'll send the information we received to the right department in Portugal," the Detective said. "The authorities need to compensate Bruno for the risk he'll take. This information is more than we expected. He's placed his life in peril."

"Will the authorities agree to move him if it becomes necessary?" Travis asked.

"They'll allow us to move and place him in protective custody."

The local authorities in Genoa let Portugal know of Dino's chilling plan to end Pearl's life in their country, a strategy that involved a web of deceit and manipulation, and a hired assassin.

When the police in Portugal heard of Dino's plan, they agreed to help.

"I'm amazed," the Detective said, his voice tinged with relief and disbelief. "I can't hold my breath for the Portuguese support. It's a momentous change."

"Ten years ago, Portugal became the first European nation to decriminalize possession of drugs, from marijuana to heroin, within their borders.

"A serious interrogation of a prisoner takes place in Jordan. If you want someone tortured, you send them to Syria. If you want someone killed, you should contact Egypt. And if you want drugs, you go to Portugal."

"Do you want to know the most effective types of scare lore?

It's the close escape from the clutches of evil," the Detective said.

"It drives home a warning better than a vivid first-person account of an averted tragedy."

"The explicit warning presented in these legends is prominent. If you keep your child out of sight, it will help.

"Kidnappers might lie in waiting anywhere. Portugal's a haven for pedophiles," he continued. "The kidnapper may drug a child to make it easier for them to alter the child's looks and smuggle him through the first exit.

"But when they smell trouble, they find the intended victim abandoned in a bathroom—half disguised with changed clothes. The kidnapper uses scissors, razors, hair dye, wigs, and clothes. And implements are used to alter the child's looks. These items stay in a bathroom stall."

The Detective removed his hat and sat by the window, looking out. "This happens worldwide, but it's more prevalent in Portugal."

"When the kidnapper tries to escape through an exit with the disguised victim, sometimes, he's caught. It's because the parent recognized the child's clothes. The kidnapper neglected to alter or forget to change his shoes. We hear horror stories of kidnapped little ones." the Detective said. "Apply your powerful skills to the fullest if you want to find Pearl."

"When in question, call me," Eagle Eye said. "I'm familiar with the law in Portugal. Make sure you work fast before they sell Pearl.

"She'll be hard to find once he moves and hides her.

"Corruption among law-enforcement agents plays a role in the success of human trade."

The same day, in the late afternoon, Travis and Joe completed their work and flew to Portugal. They were optimistic they would rescue Pearl and see Dino captured and incarcerated.

~*~*~*~

On the way to Portugal, Travis said. "There's a sad part to this mission. I do not know what part of the Algarve Dino has disappeared with Pearl. No matter how you see this, Pearl's in grave danger."

He paused. The thought of his precious wife trapped in peril made him sick.

"We're running out of time. The longer it takes to find Dino, the worse it gets for Pearl. It's my greatest concern to find her before he hides her from the locals," he said.

"We'll find her," Joe said.

Joe spends two weeks in the Algarve every summer visiting family. He's familiar with this geographical location.

On their flight to the Algarve, Joe wanted Travis to learn the region where Dino might take Pearl. "The world's best and most excellent beaches exist in Algarve, along the 200-kilometer coastline. These beaches vary from small, sheltered covers to large, endless stretches of sea-washed sand. Our quest to find Pearl will not be easy.

"Traveling along the coast from east to west, the beaches change to seasonal currents. Algarve's star attractions are along the spectacular coastline, long expanses of golden sand, and secluded coves backed by a stunning color of ochre cliffs topped by vibrant green pines.

"Each coastline's a gem, and it waits for someone to discover it. Each has a unique charm, but we may have a problem. There're ten or more beaches in Algarve," Joe said.

"The question remains: where will Dino take Pearl?"

"Wherever he takes her, we'll find it."

Joe continued. "The west coast has become more popular. The water temperature is lower than on the south coast, and the currents are more robust. We need to focus our attention there. Vigilance must take place. If someone has thoughts of suicide or intentions of murder, they might go there.

"Taking a boat ride along the coast is the best way to survey this beach. There're beaches where people get disoriented."

"It's an enormous challenge," Travis said.

"This beach at Faro Island has formed itself into a long sandpit.

"The structures are protected from the ocean's rigors, by a wall. A single road and a narrow bridge access the Island.

"You can enjoy a relaxed environment here, and you can enjoy two different beach experiences.

"On one side of the Island, the Atlantic Ocean spreads for miles and miles of sand. Conversely, you have calmer waters packed with marine life and wildlife at the Ria Formosa Natural Park. It's ideal for Dino to have two worlds at hand."

"Shall we start at Algarve and move to Faro Island?"

"You decide," Travis said.

"We can follow the officials and get reports as they receive them?"

"The officials work too slowly. Dino's callous and

brutal. And he'll kill her. He's threatened her at conflicting times. He's vengeful and holds a grudge."

"Exercise patience," Joe said.

Silence had become golden around Travis and Joe these days.

Travis prayed a brief prayer. Lord, give us answers and increase our faith.

Days later, the detective sends Travis and Joe a message about Bruno.

"Here in Genoa," he wrote. "The police authorities released Bruno from jail. I've received information that we may rescue girls. Bruno has received enough money to last until he finds a job. The police authorities moved him to a safe place in the country.

"Bruno has received a new name for his protection. We know where to find him if we need him to testify against Dino.

"I'm proud to know a fraction of what we promised went well. It's a brutal business," Eagle Eye said. "Be sure to call me if you need my help."

Travis and Joe arrived in Faro, a half-moon still kindling the night.

~*~*~*~

They'd wait till morning to go to the Algarve and rest. The darkness didn't give a hint
when they'd see the sunrise.

Travis missed Pearl and spoke loud enough to disturb Joe."

Joe's eyes flickered open for a moment, but he stayed still.

He yawned and rubbed his eyes. And while still feeling sluggish, he forced himself to touch the chilly floor barefoot.

"Losing precious time," Travis said. "I can't sleep day or night, and pretend circumstances are under control when we haven't found Pearl. We must get the latest information on Dino from the authorities.

"My body still feels heavy and numb from fatigue and lack of sleep.

"I had little sleep myself," Joe said. "But we'll go gather information this morning." He stretched his arms out and asked.

"What's the time?"

"Time to get going."

The police department informed them that a couple named Dino and Pearl had taken a taxi.

"Good news," Joe said. "This officer handed us a basket of goodies. We have two witnesses. We can call on them if we need to contact these folks."

They tasted grace, and they'll take back what belonged to Travis.

Sweat trickled down Travis's face. His fists curled, making his knuckles turn white and creating a tight knot in his stomach. "Pearl's close by, but where? Dino has retribution on his mind." A tear rolled down his cheek at the thought.

"Finding Pearl will take time," Travis said. He jumped into the boat and sat in silence while Joe pulled out.

"Mark Twain once said: 'My problem's not what's difficult to understand in the Bible. But what I understand is what troubles me.' The same truth applies to me," Travis said, reflecting on his own struggles and understanding of the situation.

"As we learn His word," Joe said. "The Holy Spirit enlightens us. Transformation occurs when a person becomes obedient to what he has learned.

"In those dark moments, God might make His greatest attribute known. We won't have peace if we don't allow God's presence in our lives."

A broken man, Travis disregarded God's hand at work and accepted that he couldn't find peace without

Pearl.

~*~*~*~

He urged Pearl to walk along the shoreline.

"On a day like this, beachgoers stroll the beach," he said.

A storm ready to break fed Pearl's fears. She glanced at the sky. The low clouds gathered over the mountains.

"I know violent storms spring from the remotest places," she said. "I heard a weather report this morning. There's a storm headed this way."

"We'll come back in if the storm gets wicked.

She joined him with reluctance.

In a matter of minutes, the sky exploded with lightning. A fast-moving storm arrived. "There's little to fear. Dino's here," he said.

The clap of thunder reverberated from the mountaintop to the mountain pass. Without warning, another clap of thunder sounded like the sky might spin out of control on a downward course. A flash of lightning lit the entire sky.

The torrential rain lashed onto solid sheets of water and drenched her in a second. Pearl cried out in fear. Blinded and choked by the rain, she overlooked the hand, grabbing her arm and pulling her back.

But she clung to it. She shuddered. Her legs buckled. Dino swept her into his arms as he staggered into the small bungalow he'd rented. He fought the relentless wall of rain at every step.

Pearl remained dazed. She hadn't experienced such ferocious weather before. She reached the bungalow with help from her captor, who supported her in his arms.

Dino said it in a soft voice. "I'll light a fire, and you must change out of those wet clothes, or you'll get sicker than a dog. There are two thin towels in the bathroom. Wrap yourself in one. It'll help."

Pearl's teeth chattered as she stripped off her sodden clothes, her body shivering from the cold. It surprised her to learn that Dino had saved her from the storm, his actions revealing a side of him she hadn't expected.

Pearl stretched out her grateful hands to the warmth of the fire. In contrast, Dino set their soaked clothes out to dry.

"There," he said and smiled. "It'll take minutes for them to dry. In the meantime, I'll get you a hot drink."

The current setting scared her more than the ordeal she'd experienced. Conscious of the looks of intimacy this problem brought, the thin towel blankets they wore made her tremble.

When Dino appeared with the hot chocolate, his glance looked innocent. Dino seemed to want to put her at ease.

He sipped the hot chocolate and said, "I'm as upset as you." He touched her shoulder. "I've respected your emotions and haven't allowed men to hassle you. His mouth twisted to form a wry expression.

"I underestimated this storm. I ought to have brought you inside out of danger long before it hit." Dino went on and on, expressing regret for his past actions.

Pearl turned him off, and she became insensitive to his words. The rain beating on the roof faded into the distance. It mingled with the far-off echo of his deep, raspy voice. The fireplace's heat and sips of the soothing drink relaxed her, and she fell asleep.

Dino prattled on; his eyes fixed on the view before him. Pearl was fast asleep on the sofa with a towel wrapped around her, which created an unusual mood. His eyes rested on her body. He behaved like a man with wicked intentions.

Dino admitted to himself what his heart had shown him long ago.

Pearl slept and snubbed his affection, but he continued to reveal his heart to her.

"Yes," he said. "I've cherished you from the first day I saw you with your mother."

When no answer came, he lifted her into his arms and carried her into the bedroom. Pearl heard the slam of a door, and her body stiffened.

Her sleepy eyes focused on the intended offense. She shivered and sensed a wrong had taken place. She felt like she was coming out of a trance.

"Let go of me!" she yelled and kicked. Dino dropped her. Pearl scrambled to her feet and wobbled her way into the front room.

"Dino must have drugged me," she whispered.

"You're an expert on corruption, misery, and lies," she shouted.

"Countless decent changes occur in this world but evil magnifies and overwhelms you."

Dino ran his fingers through his messy hair and sat cross-legged on the sofa. His narrow eyes studied her with edginess. "I'm surprised at your reaction after I saved you from the storm. Lightning might've hit you when you fell. You're the most ungrateful woman I've ever met."

Pearl looked over and stared into his angry face.

Dino avoided her eyes. Dino had fought with his heart, but he didn't conquer destiny.

Pearl swallowed her discontent, gripped the arms of her chair, and her lip quivered. Pearl spoke in a gravelly voice and stared at Dino. "Take me back home to my husband."

The fury in his eyes meant he'd reverted to his original plan. Dino stayed busy on his phone for the rest of the day and evening.

"Night fell and filled me with fear and disgust. I'm horrified by the mystery that surrounds this place. And Dino holding me captive makes me fear more than the darkness or the dank and slimy walls."

Pearl's head ached, and she had an enormous thirst and felt dehydrated. "I'm reluctant to touch the water jug Dino set before me for fear I'll drink contaminated water." She tiptoed to where Dino set the jug and emptied it half to make him think she drank the water.

I heard footsteps outside and loud voices. I sprang to my feet in sudden terror. "The end has arrived for me. I must collect myself and not allow him to see my fear." I pretended to sleep, although I claimed reasons to pull an all-nighter.

While Pearl ruminated on her fate, she wept. "Lord, it's over for me. The obvious has come upon me. I can't contact Travis, and I have little hope I'll see him anew," Pearl fixed her eyes on the window. The outside darkness scared her, and she covered her head with the blanket.

Pearl continued her conversation with the Lord in a whisper. "Lord, I miss Travis's warm embrace, his tender lips. I miss his voice. Lord, please allow me to embrace my husband again and tell him I belong to him."

Travis, my dear husband, yet we're miles apart; you're on my mind each morning. Deep within my soul, I hear your call. I can't forget your smile, and I miss your tender voice. We've shared beautiful remembrances. If we don't meet again, your name will linger on my lips until my last breath.

I know Dino's regard for me has turned to aversion. I've become an object of hatred. And his obsession with taking retribution has driven his insanity over the edge. But, Lord, let him come to his senses before it's too late. And what comes after? I do not know, she thought.

Pearl buried her face in the pillow on this uncertain night and wept until sheer exhaustion claimed her.

Morning came, and she bounced out of bed with relief. She was still alive.

Dino gathered with his men outside the bungalow.

She covered her mouth with her hand. "No place to

run or hide," she whispered. Pearl's fears forced her back into bed. "I heard these men last night. They've returned," Pearl murmured.

The door sprang open. A frantic or irrational person appeared and shouted, "Oh, Amore!" Dino said, anguish engraved on his face. Pearl's body stiffened when she heard the name Amore. He took hold of the jug and shook it.

Pearl closed her eyes. Dino must've believed I drank water from the jug and was dead. She reflected on what he might plan next and remained silent.

Dino stood at the foot of the bed and gawked. He dragged his attention from Pearl to his men, aware they stood at the doorway, staring. Dino's enormous eyes popped out, and he whirled in fury.

"Go empty this jug and fill it with fresh water!" he said, addressing the men standing at the doorway.

Pearl's eyes flew wide open. I must not let him know I've seen movement outside the window. These men came to carry me to my resting place.

She stayed tense and horrified. Pearl wiped the tears, which blurred her vision.

Dino stared at Pearl with an evil look. His haunting eyes appeared wicked—the worst she'd seen. It was spine-chilling.

Lord, I'm facing evil straight in the eye, but will I live to tell the story? Dino looks as if someone has sucked the blood out of his body.

Oh, Jesus, my soul cries out. I'm so scared. Please get me out of here, Lord. I know Dino can't steal my soul because it belongs to you. Please help me, Lord.

"I must cling to my faith," she whispered. "Lord, I'm shaking like a leaf," she said, shivering. "I must muster enough courage to escape. Lord, I grasp my hands in agony for Travis. An unbearable sense of emptiness and fear overwhelms me."

Unable to prevent this inevitable event, Pearl

surrendered and responded as if the world had ended. I'm fortunate to have escaped death last night, but I will give to Dino's plan today. Thank you, Lord, for bringing me to a new discernment.

Pearl prayed, "Lord, I'm broken and have lost my way. Hope's gone. I hear a storm raging in the distance calling my name."

Dino chased his men away.

"Please take me to see a doctor. I'm sick," she said.

"Oh, my discontented sojourner, you won't need a doctor where we're going," Dino said with a dismissive wave of his hand.

"Prepare for a long and vague journey. Your spirit and soul will taste freedom," he said, staring at her.

"I won't allow your weakness to ruin my plans this time. Sorry, but I'm afraid your demand is not one I can honor."

Her rapid, shallow breathing frightened her. Her heart might fail at any moment.

"Let's go for a walk along the coastline, and I'll give you the history of the Algarve," Dino said.

"I can't walk far," she said.

"Get motivated," he said. "Algarve's a small region with a dense population. I'm intrigued by this place; Algarve's a short drive to places where you can disappear for hours without a view of a house, hamlet, or town."

"Alvor's one of Algarve's most popular destinations, set for weddings," Dino said, gazing at Pearl.

Pearl looked away. Dino kept taunting her.

"The Rio de Formosa stretches from Faro past Tavira, with low-barrier islands, lagoons, and waterways.

"I've heard someone drown in a lagoon, and they never found the body," Dino said.

"We must go explore the hills first."

Pearl's heartbeat against her ribs. She fought to mask the images of this nightmare before it engulfed her.

"Dino, I'm afraid I can't manage the long walk," she said.

Dino paid little attention to her and spoke in a hasty and rough voice with an Italian accent.

"We can walk the hills, study the lagoons, drive to a quiet place, or go to a little chapel and get married."

"I'd accept death before I'd marry you," she blurted out.

"Okay, prepare for the fun. Before the major event, I'm taking you to visit a sea infested with jellyfish. You'll experience the pain of a sting from a jellyfish."

Dino will implement his threats if he sets his mind to it.

Dino stood in front of her and stared. "Do you want a drink of water?" Dino asked her with a smile.

She nodded.

"I won't let you die of thirst before the major event. You'll soon face deep water—undrinkable water—and it won't quench your thirst," he said, gesturing with his hands.

"You'll finish what you started back in Genoa. It's a little payback for what you've made me suffer. I struggled to prove my innocence. But no thanks to you, I might've spent my life in prison without a graceful gesture from you."

Dino paused for a second and stared at Pearl and mumbled, "Ora is il grande tempo finire ti lavoro, Mi Amoro."

Motionless, she stood, straining her eyes and ears.

After no reaction from Pearl, Dino said. "I'll explain myself. Remember the plan you concocted back in Italy? I'll make sure it works this time."

It gave Dino immense pleasure to see the horror in Pearl's eyes.

"You can imagine the plan I have designed for you." Dino's smile appeared pasted on his face. "I'm glad you get the picture. You love pulling pranks. You'll try it again, and

I assure you, you'll get the job done this time. I've chosen to make this clear to Travis.

"When he receives the articles published in the Local Newspaper of Genoa, it'll be clear you've been declared dead, and he'll recognize it as old news. But he'll experience the same agony as I did. It's fair, and I know you'll agree with me."

Dino strolled to where Pearl sat, rested his arm on her right shoulder, and said. "Amore, you must understand; the law can't charge me over this. If you recall, you died a long time ago. A person can't die twice. According to records, the police authorities can't put me on trial for your death because you don't exist."

Pearl's mouth dropped open, and she shook her head in horror. Her body quivered, and fear surged through her.

Dino strolled away to allow her to consider her fate.

Fear has occupied my mind. The notion of Dino thrusting me into the sea and the terror Travis may experience have taken a toll on me. Enormous stuff to endure, she thought.

Pearl closed her eyes, her face pale and tense. Lord, I ask for forgiveness if I've caused Dino any anguish that has driven him to this. Please give him compassion for others. You're a God of mercy.

Please protect my dear husband and comfort him. I trust you will do this for me. Please give him peace and have mercy on me. Rivers of water run from my eyes because of Dino's anger toward me. Please replace it with forgiveness.

Father in heaven, please forgive me if to close I lean my heart on you. Pearl kept her eyes closed. She drew a sharp breath when she looked up and saw Dino standing before her.

Every move and word made Dino a lightning rod.

"Try to sleep," Dino said. "You'll need your strength.

Dino stared at her and said, "You're not the innocent girl of long ago. I've done so much for you. Being submissive is the least you can do. Here's the glass of water I promised you," he said, threw it in her face, and left with approval.

Pearl gasped for air. Her body trembled with fear. "The end has arrived," she thought.

CHAPTER 14~THE FINAL SHOT

The frosty day and the sharp air have made me queasy. Then the cheapskate rented a shoddy motel, Pearl thought.

Pearl noticed one of Dino's men or business partners talking to him. They shook hands, and their gestures meant they agreed.

The hairy man came into the room and went to talk to Pearl on the sofa. He eyed her with enticement. Dino smiled, and Pearl looked at him in disgust.

Dino walked behind the hairy man with a smile. "You want her? Take her," he said. "I promise, she's the same price today or tomorrow."

The man nodded approval and reached out for Pearl's arm.

Dino's fat grin on his face got wider.

Pearl kicked, screamed, and scratched his face. The man looked shocked and backed off, holding his face. He pulled out a knife.

Dino rushed and slammed him against the wall. Dino wrapped his arm behind his back, pulling and twisting until he dropped the knife.

"If I can't explain this to my wife, I'm coming after you," he said.

"I told you she's ferocious," Dino said. The man extended his hand, and Dino turned over his accepted money. "She's a wild and crazy woman," he said and hurried away.

Pearl felt dirty. "Lord, protect me from this inferno,"

she muttered.

"I'm not finished here. I'll make a fortune with you," Dino said.

"Over my dead body," Pearl said.

"I'll make more than enough to pay for my expenses on this trip." Dino's lip curled, and his head tilted and shrugged.

"You wait and see. Get ready. One of the finest restaurants expects us tonight."

"I don't intend to step out in public with you, no matter how severe the consequences," she said.

"Let me set you straight on this. You're going. You better wash and comb your hair unless you want to appear like a slob."

"This appointment for dinner has the potential to increase my clients and make a good impression."

"You're a deranged man," she said.

Dino turned around and slapped her. "I'm not taking any backtalk from you. Please don't argue with me. I couldn't care less about your opinion. You get it!" He reached for her ear, twisted as hard as he could, dragged her to the bathroom, and said, "Get ready."

Pearl clenched her teeth to keep from crying.

"Travis will die by nightfall," Dino blurted out.

"Oh, no, you can't kill him! You promised!"

"Get ready. I'll be right outside making calls."

"The secret to happiness is freedom, and courage exists in the strength to resist fear." Minutes later, she strolled to the window, her eyes resting on a cisalpine sparrow flying unrestricted.

Pearl gathered the courage to run to a nearby house to seek help. She opened the door, and there stood Dino, his phone pinned to his ear.

Dino turned around and grabbed her arm. "What's your business out here?"

"I'll cooperate with you, she said, seized by fear."

Dino released her, and she slammed the door in his face. With a sinking sense of despair, she dragged herself back to the sofa.

It's too late to escape. This bird can't fly. I don't have the courage or strength, and Dino's scheduling appointments for me. He'll drug me, and I'll turn into a prostitute, and he'll be my pimp. I'll become addicted to drugs and will not be fit to go back home to Travis.

"Lord, send someone to help me before this happens," she whispered. A whimper of despair escaped her lips, and she collapsed on the sofa.

Dino stepped back in and set his phone on the dresser. "A change of plans," he said. "It's best if the big guy comes to visit you. And you better behave. I'm going out of town. This gentleman will protect you while I'm gone. When I return, prepare to move to another motel."

Pearl's lips quivered.

She tried running out the door. With a tight grip on her arm, Dino said, "You're worth a fortune. You won't rob me of this wealth. I'm not pleased to leave you with a stranger, but I'm afraid I must take a day or two off to recover from your untamed behavior. I won't stay away a minute longer than necessary."

I better get away before someone else arrives, she thought.

Pearl glanced out the window and saw a new Lexus pull into the driveway.

"Oh, no," she said. She stroked her hair behind her ear, and terror swept through her body.

The man parked the car, and a six-foot-plus obese man knocked. Dino opened the door and showed him respect. They glanced at each other and bumped elbows as Dino hurried out.

The cheerful fat man walked in and greeted Pearl with a "Hello, doll." He eyed her from top to bottom, and his eyes pierced hers.

"Fabulous," he said, giving her a wicked wink.

The sleaze bag drawled.

A gorgeous woman like you needs a handsome and generous man like me.

Pearl's heart pounded. He'll take me in his arms and try to kiss me in another moment. "He's a pervert," she whispered. She flew to the bathroom, where she hid Dino's gun—the gun that he lost in the helicopter.

The fat man chuckled.

Pearl returned in a determined spirit. "Get out," she said, pointing the gun at his head.

"Honey, we can talk this over a drink," he said, approaching her.

"Get out, or I'll shoot you. I'm not joking."

The fat man continued to get closer. "A nice young lady won't shoot an unarmed man."

A shot rang out. The fat man dashed toward the door, leaving his hat with a bullet hole in the floor. But before he left, he said, "You've made a mistake revolting people make, and they pay with their lives."

"Get out!" She said.

Pearl's eyes filled with tears, and she didn't notice the glare he gave her, one of hostility.

Pearl sat on the edge of the bed and sobbed in despair. She stared at the hat with a hole in the brim and inhaled a deep, quivering breath. "I must get rid of the evidence," Pearl said. She kicked the hat out of the door. The hat landed on a tree branch, where it dangled. She pulled the door shut behind her and locked it.

Darkness approached. Pearl strolled to the window and strained to see through the obscurity. The black barrier of the hill remained visible. A thin glitter from the new-risen moon touched the dancing tops of the trees.

Fighting the sobs that rose in her throat, she hurried to the door. "I must take off before someone else comes." But before she ran off, another fear gripped her soul. Pearl made a quick move and hid the gun.

"I came back for my phone." He looked around and asked, "Where's the big guy?"

"I told him my body is not for sale. I scratched his face and kicked him out the door. The fat man went home crying to momma."

Dino went crazy. Dino yanked her hair, jerked her head, and she went flying, hitting her forehead against a door stopper. "Do you know what you have done? You have put us both in danger. I ought to kill you and remove you from my life."

Dino appeared scared and said, "Hurry, let's go before he returns."

Her bleeding came from her eyebrow. Dazed and injured, Pearl needed attention. Instead, she turned into a brave captive with no more fear. She went into a fury and shouted into his face.

"Among all the sleazy and dirty conduct, you've engaged in, this deed is the lowest."

"Shut your mouth, woman! I can't think." He said, giving her a threatening glare.

A wise person stays silent, she thought.

Dino continued to gather his possessions.

Pearl followed Dino's orders for a time, fearing the obese man might return.

~*~*~*~

Dino moved five miles to Motel Parque Algario. There, he continued his calling for potential customers.

"I will replenish lost revenue," Dino said. "I need money."

Her thoughts reverted to her husband. I know Travis has set out in search of me. He's not sitting around waiting for Dino's men. Dino can't harm him anymore.

"A powerful man is coming, and he demands obedience." Dino

shook her by the shoulders. "Make him a happy

man."

"I disapprove of your lechers," she said. "I have no intention of pleasing them."

"Let me warn you. You must please this man, or you're dead.

A brief time later, another man met Dino. "I know the routine," she whispered as Dino shook hands with the pervert.

Travis and Joe advanced along the coast with a lucid blue sky on this delightful day.

They saw a group of men standing in the marina. Amid the group of men, Dino stood out, looking proud."

Travis fought to keep his hands steady. His rapid pulse frightened him. Streams of sweat cascaded off his unshaven face. Thoughts of Pearl filled his mind. He spent moments surveying the marina but didn't see Pearl. His forehead creased, and a knot formed in his stomach.

"What's wrong?" He asked. "Men surround Dino, meeting his every need with a finger snap. But where's Pearl?"

"Let's pull over and watch," Joe said. "It'll give us a chance to watch their activity. I'm sure Pearl's somewhere nearby."

They sat and waited. The tightness in Travis's gut rose. His cheeks turned red angrily, and his hands trembled to hold the binoculars. The fear in the pit of my stomach increases with every moment.

"Stay calm," Joe said. "We're nearing finding Pearl."

They took turns watching the men on the boat dock through binoculars for 35 minutes.

Joe handed Travis the binoculars. "The boat's a piece of junk. Dino climbed into the boat and started the engine. His men moved behind the bolder, watching Dino drive it around in tight circles, making sharp turns."

"I guess he's on a test drive," Joe said.

"Dino has sailed out of sight, but there's no sign of Pearl."

Travis's heart slammed against his ribs. He stared at the boat as it disappeared, and his lips tightened into a thin line. "Lord," he prayed, "Dino has murder on his mind. Please bring Pearl back," he whispered.

"We should've made our move when we first recognized him." His voice quivered. "Dino will not return."

"Dino will return," Joe said. "Pearl's not with him."

"How much of Dino's cruelty can she take?" He closed his eyes to block out the thoughts.

Fifteen minutes had expired when Dino pulled back to the harbor. Dino's men stepped out to meet him.

Dino jumped out, smiled, and tapped the boat on the side. He waved to the fifth man in a van, who appeared with Pearl by his side.

"Look, there's Pearl," Travis gasped. "Let's go get her."

"Let's wait," Joe said, grabbed his excited friend's arm, and pulled him back. "The small boat can't accommodate five men and Pearl. Let's wait."

An itch on my back has traveled to my neck, Travis said. And he spoke with words far more broken than he imagined possible. "If Dino leaves with Pearl, we'll lose the opportunity to save her for the second time."

These challenges of fear go deep. Will I find my way to the surface? He thought as he grew anxious.

Dino's men lifted Pearl into the small boat.

Travis sensed a sharp pain in the palm of his hands. He noticed his nails digging sharp pinpricks into his skin.

"Dino has dismissed his men," Joe said. "They have moved away from the boat."

Dino strapped on a life jacket without offering Pearl one. He checked the slim-shape object on his side. The four men jumped into the van and drove away.

"He intends to intimidate Pearl," Travis said.

"Time to move in," Joe said.

A shot of adrenaline surged through Travis's veins as he sprang into action. "Lord, I know how Dino works. From the depths of my soul, I call on you, Lord, to hear my cry for help."

Dino noticed Travis coming toward the dock and grabbed Pearl with one hand while he backed the boat out. Pearl attacked him, screamed at the top of her lungs, and fought to jump out. But he pulled her back, a wicked snarl across his lips while she screamed and clawed at him.

"You're not going anywhere," Dino said. "People who treat me as a fool seldom get away with it. There're consequences for what you've done."

Pearl suffered a bruised arm from his firm grip. He held on to her with one hand and maneuvered the boat with the other. The outlines of Travis and Joe on the pier faded as the craft advanced.

Minutes passed, and the engine went silent. Pearl shivered when she heard Dino's laughter.

Dino raised his hands in the air in victory. He turned his attention away from Pearl for a
minute. She glanced at him, and her eyes rested on his gun and keys for a second. Pearl lunged and grabbed the keys from the ignition.

"You won't hold me back this time," she cried. Pearl threw the keys into the water before he grabbed her.

She experienced the icy metal of his gun resting against the side of her face. "See what you've done. My plans have changed," he said. His voice roared in her ear. "You've badgered me for the last time. I must kill you and sail away without you!"

Dino yelled at the top of his lungs toward the distant shore.

"Ancora una volta ho vinto, non si sarà mai proprio lei, Travis."

Pearl heard him shout it in English. "One more time, Travis, I've won! Pearl's mine! And I can protect her or destroy her."

Dino turned to face Pearl and said, "You're as deceitful as thin ice. You have made your biggest mistake. These actions you've taken have given great strength to an old emotion within me. I provided, protected, and lavished you with gifts, but you didn't appreciate it. If I can't have you, neither can Travis."

Dino's hard breathing increased. "We must leave this place together and go to our resting place."

"I have unfinished business and am not prepared to die."

"Business, what business?" Dino asked. He pointed the weapon at Pearl and pulled the trigger, but he missed her head by inches.

The loud noise of the gunfire pierced her ear. People ran for cover on the beach, causing disarray.

"Pearl!" Travis screamed above the roar of the engine.

A hundred meters away was a kind angler who offered the keys to his boat. "Alert the authorities and the Coast Guard. Give them the location," Joe told the angler.

"Joe drove. Once on the way, Joe pressed the boat's control to go faster.

Dino saw the craft get closer and closer.

"Faster, faster," Travis said.

"This boat's old and slow. Twenty-five miles per hour is what I can get from this antique, but I'm grateful."

Dino aimed and fired various rounds. Joe focused on the vessel straight ahead, even when a bullet grazed his arm. He ignored the intensity of his injury.

"Lord, we depend on you," Joe prayed.

"Prayer after prayer, we hope, but we receive no change. I spend my time begging and crying out for Pearl's release and safety, but the chaos continues. Strengthen us to advance with courage," Travis prayed.

The status between Dino and Pearl remained intense. His eyes burned in his dark face.

Dino turned and glared at Pearl. Pearl reached into her pocket and pulled out a small handgun. The revolver she'd kept hidden from Dino after it fell out of his pocket in the helicopter. The same firearm Pearl used on Dino's potential customers.

"Fear no longer has power over me," she said.

Pearl pointed the gun at his heart. "Dino, you're a man with a soul stained with innocent blood. Your lips speak falsehood. Travis hoped you'd choose the right path, but we never saw a change in you. You've reached the end, as I have."

Dino's eyes widened when he learned Pearl controlled this situation. "My handgun," he said. "You found my handgun." Dino reached out to grab it.

With a low spirit and little energy, she yelled, "Stop! I'm not playing your game anymore."

Dino sniggered. "It takes more than willpower to pull the trigger. Besides, I can draw my gun faster than you can shoot."

"This is my game, and it'll end when I say it's over. Before I kill you, let's answer each other's questions.

"I lost my mother early, and I miss her. The records show she died four years ago. Who killed my mother?" Pearl asked.

With great enthusiasm, Dino said. "I laid Bella to rest. Bruno buried her at the base of a mountain. The mountain she visited often. She has a superb view of the city below.

Pearl lost her composure and fired a shot but missed. "Oh, my magnificent mountain, you've ripped my heart by taking someone I loved. She belonged to me, and she's gone." Pearl grieved, and her eyes flooded with tears.

Pearl continued to whimper.

"I picked out her resting place," Dino said with smugness and self-confidence. "During our existence, we meet people with negative attitudes. It's a tricky business to have a good relationship with old nags."

"You took her from her husband and detained and killed her."

"It's known how I run my business. The minute any girl steps into my pad, I have power over them. And I have the privilege of carrying whatever comes to mind with them. You're ungrateful. Bella lived a pleasant life before her death.

"And as far as you're concerned, from the first time I saw you with your mother, I knew you'd someday become part of my belongings. Your presence is still, by far, the most unpredictable.

You're the youngest to step into my pad and live this long. But you have no reason to complain.

"Well," Dino said, shrugging. "I must confess, I hired Bruno to kill her. I plan to bring you to my pad and make you my queen, little miss ungrateful. But you paid little attention to our relationship."

She was full of grief and anger. "A relationship between a pimp and a prisoner. What makes you assume friendship can exist with someone who preys on the young? Destroys lives and sells or buys girls as young as eight years of age," she said. "It's immoral."

"I needed money," he said. "But you ought to have made matters easier. If you had cooperated with me and performed, the future might've changed. But you worked against me."

"By performing, you mean I must embrace your perverted customers. You'd have to kill me first."

"There's another incident; I will confess. I feared you'd find a boyfriend before I made you mine. So, I told your father a lie about the wild boy in your neighborhood."

Pearl learned Dino had victimized her father, too.

"I blame you for my father's heart attack. Take the thought to your grave."

Dino continued to confess and ignored her broken heart. "I trust your father's rage made you run away. You made the right decision." he said smiling, "I waited for you. Tu sei una stell—la mia stella."

"How dare you call me your star!" she said. "Call me your worst enemy. And while we're handling this with truth, respond to my grievances. You considered yourself privileged in my father's house. You ransacked my dad's bedroom. And you had a brainstorming idea for showering in his home. You're a despicable person."

"You should be careful in the choice of words you use. Or you'll question why I've ripped out your tongue."

"You've destroyed my family, killed my father and mother, and shattered my life. You've tried to kill Travis, the person I love most. Days ago, you set out to sell me to your predator friends."

Pearl kept her voice calm and said, "You robbed me of a blissful life with my husband, but you'll never steal my soul. And I'll take pleasure in killing you.

Dino panicked and shot Pearl in the chest before she acted.

Travis heard a shot over the roar of the engines and saw Pearl fall forward on Dino. They vanished underneath the craft boat, and Travis heard another gunshot.

Joe pulled the boat craft alongside Dino's. Travis leaped into the vessel and noticed Pearl, unconscious, stretched out on the boat floor. A handgun rested on the floor, inches from her.

"Pearl!" Travis screamed and fell to his knees in agony. He held her in his arms and made sure she was alive by checking her pulse.

Dino held his pistol upward in his hand and had a snarl on his face. He had failed to reload and searched his pockets for ammunition. He cursed in Italian. Dino pulled the trigger but missed Travis.

Travis heard the clang of Dino's pistol falling to the floor. He ignored Dino's dying curses and last breath.

Seconds later, the Italian Coast Guard arrived. Travis looked on as doctors and sailors hoisted Pearl on board to stabilize her. The Coast Guard loaded Joe to treat his wound.

Travis drove the boat back to the owner. When he arrived at the hospital to check on
Pearl, he saw the giant red welts on her wrists where Dino had bound her.

"Please forgive me," He said. "I'm so sorry you've experienced such a frightful ordeal." He cupped her hands with his, kissed them, and remained beside her for the rest of her hospital stay. Dino had shot Pearl inches above her heart.

Days later, he heard Pearl whisper. "I missed you, Travis."

"Thank you, Lord," he said, cupping her face and kissing her. I'm grateful you've survived. His voice quivered. "I missed you too."

Travis kissed her. She missed his loving nature.

"Oh, Travis," she said. "I prayed for this moment."

Travis pressed his hand against her face and felt the hot tears on her cheek.

She whispered, "Amazing Grace. Our faith has brought us through."

"Yes, He's a faithful God. He never deserted us, not for a minute.

"Honey, the nightmare has ended. Dino met his fate. You're free at last—no more days of terror. The days of Grace have arrived.

"All's well with my soul. God's still in control. Those trusting in the Lord will find new strength," Travis said. "Whatever deep waters of tragedy and sorrow we face, God's with us, and He'll keep us from drowning."

"Travis," Pearl whispered, "Dino's dead, but not by my hand. My gun jammed." she said and then fell asleep.

So, who shot Dino? It is a mystery we may never solve.

A young runaway survived the clutches of evil, and a young man endured the rages of war, both saved by Grace.

Thank you, Holy God. Your power's made perfect in my weakness.

The End